All the Rest of Her Days

A novel by

Jane F. McCarthy

Jane F. McCarthy

To Mary Elizabeth, Eileen and Kate

To Mary Elizabeth, Eileen and Kate

Acknowledgements

There are many people who shared their knowledge of the written word with me and showed me how to turn the words into stories. To my friends and mentors, Jane Maxson and Betty Cotter, who read the manuscript and gave me invaluable editorial and grammatical advice and provided consistent support in this regard. To Jane Goodger who provided me with her verbal and written editorial advice, the hard part and the easy part. To Ann Fessler whose book THE *GIRLS WHO WENT AWAY,* gave me insight into the lives of girls who surrendered their children for adoption. To the members of the Neighborhood Guild Creative Writing Group for being my friends and fellow writers. To my husband, Gerry, for his invaluable computer support and being my ally through our journey.

"without the hurt the heart is hollow"
From *Try to Remember*

Prologue

After years of searching and several dead ends he finally had a name and telephone number. Was this her? It had to be. But what if it wasn't? He had woven his way through his background. The final thread was his last hope.

Many times he picked up the phone, held it in his hand and, too afraid of rejection, hung up before dialing. He would hold onto the receiver for a moment and then put the paper back in his pocket and forget for another day. Today was different; it was his birthday.

On the other side of the Atlantic, in Peabody, Massachusetts, Maggie Porter Carlson drove into her driveway, turned off the ignition, gathered up the packages on the passenger seat and headed for her house. Even now, thirty years later, she still wondered where he was and if he was safe. She knew she would always wonder.

As she unlocked the door she heard the phone ring. Her first thought was to let the answering machine pick it up. Then, deciding maybe it was her younger daughter, Emma, needing a ride home from ballet class, she answered it.

"Hello."

"Is this Maggie Porter?" said the voice on the other end.

"Yes, my name is Maggie, but it's Porter-Carlson now."

His search was over. He had found her. He needed to ask one question. Silence prevailed. He cleared his throat and said, "Does September 2, 1957 mean anything to you?"

PART ONE

Chapter One

✎

Sitting on the edge of her bed Maggie Porter was unable to control her quivering body as tears tumbled down her cheeks leaving a salty taste in the corners of her mouth. Up until now her life had been full of excitement and anticipation of things to come but she did not count on this; a situation that at sixteen years old would have ramifications for the rest of her life. How long could she contain her secret and how long did she have before telling her parents the awful truth?

The yellow buses stood in the parking lot of Brant High waiting for their passengers to arrive to take them home for the last run of the school year. Maggie raced down the steps with her best friend, Karen, close by. Maggie slipped her pony tail holder off and shook her honey colored hair loose. Her right arm shot upward as she flashed her broad smile and extended a wave to teachers standing along the grass. Teachers were pleased when Maggie was in their class; she had a way of engaging her friends in discussions. To Maggie everything was possible and nothing was impossible.

Maggie turned to Karen, "Do you believe our sophomore year is over and we have all summer together? You and I have to see *The King and I* and sleepover at each other's houses."

"What are your doing for the summer?" asked Karen.

"Camp for four weeks, my learners permit, volunteering for Miss Simpson at the library during story hour and in September I'm taking the honors English class with Mr. Brooks. He already told me. We're halfway through high school, Karen. Just imagine."

"I could never go to camp. Too many bugs and too many kids. I'll probably end up working for my father again in his boring drugstore."

"It's not so bad, Karen. At least you get free sodas. And you get to see Billy Walsh."

"Billy Walsh doesn't even know I'm alive."

Maggie slid her arm through Karen's. "I think Billy Walsh likes you. I see the way he looks at you."

Karen twisted her brown curls between her thumb and finger. "Do you think so?"

"Of course. I bet he asks you out this summer."

"And I bet George Cooper asks you out."

"If that happens and all my summer plans happen, I'll be the luckiest girl alive."

The girls boarded the school bus; Maggie's stop was first on the route. She said goodbye to Karen promising to call her that evening. Maggie walked to her house watching Mrs. Gendron unload her station wagon of groceries while her son rode his tricycle down the driveway. She turned the corner to see Mrs. King sitting on the front steps of her house with a cigarette in one hand and a cup of coffee in the other waiting for the school bus to drop off her seven-year-old twins; she waved to Maggie. Mrs. Barrett came by pushing a baby carriage along the sidewalk while her toddler daughter hung on to the handle. Occasionally, Maggie baby sat for these children.

Maggie's summer went as planned except for the absence of an invitation from George Cooper to go out on a date. Undaunted,

Maggie prevailed knowing she would see him now that school started and the fall dance for juniors and seniors was coming up. Maggie had chosen two dresses for the occasion but could not make up her mind which one she would wear. Should it be the mauve colored one delicately dotted with black polka dots with a modest V neck line and black cummerbund or the cherry red one dotted with small white polka dots and a white sash, cap sleeves and a full skirt? Both dresses accentuated her tiny waist and slim frame. She chose her new black flats that would be good for dancing. Once the dress decision was made she could work on getting rid of the jitters at the prospect of dancing with handsome George Cooper who smiled at her every time they passed each other in the hallway at school and one time he even winked at her.

One day in the cafeteria he stood so close to her she thought she would faint. "Hi," he said running a hand through his dark brown hair. Maggie looked up into his handsome face; he had a square jaw, thin lips that were smiling and brown eyes that stared at her.

"Hi," Maggie said flashing her big smile and smoothing her poodle skirt.

"Going to the dance Saturday night?" George asked loosening the collar of his tan, button down shirt.

"I am."

"Good, I'll see you there."

Maggie moved through the line in the cafeteria trying to control her heart pounding in her chest.

Karen arrived Saturday afternoon. The teenagers hurried to Maggie's bedroom to begin their preparation for the big event. Maggie closed the bedroom door. Karen laid her dress carefully on the bed.

"Karen, what do you think?" Maggie asked displaying both dresses.

"Definitely the red one. Make it easier for George to find you. I have some rouge. Mom bought it for me. She said 'only use a little'. We can try it out. Daddy refuses to let me wear lipstick. He only agreed to the rouge because Mom said it was fine."

"My father says the same thing about lipstick too but it will be fun wearing the rouge. What if George doesn't ask me to dance? I'll just die if he doesn't."

"He will, I just know it. Just like I'm sure Billy Walsh will ask me. He even said so. Here, I bought this for you." Karen handed Maggie a necklace with a four-leaf clover charm dangling from the end. "It will bring you luck."

"Karen, you are the best friend of all," said Maggie as she put the four-leaf clover around her neck and applied the rouge to her cheekbones which accentuated her flawless skin and complimented her blue eyes. "Come on, supper's ready."

After supper Maggie's mother drove the girls to the dance. They slid in the front seat next to her, their billowing dresses almost occluding their vision.

As they entered the auditorium the visceral beats of music greeted them, strobe lights circled above them, hands beckoned to them, laughter and voices competed with each other and the music. Maggie stood with her hands clasped in front of her, her eyes wide; she felt electricity crawl under her skin. At that moment she felt a large hand on her shoulder, she turned and George Cooper asked her to dance. Her heart skipped a beat and before she could say yes he put his arm around her waist and led her to the dance floor where the red dress swung with their every move. Maggie's head came just under George's chin, her lips brushing up against his throat, her hand resting on his broad shoulder. They danced to Fats Domino's rendition of *Blueberry Hill*. Maggie and George danced every dance together and at the end of the last dance George dipped Maggie back holding her tight and kissed her on the lips. Maggie felt lightheaded. They stood upright and George twirled Maggie around lifting her off her feet their laughter lasting until the crowd dispersed. George asked Maggie to go out the following Friday night; she accepted and their courtship began.

Friday was bowling night. Maggie and George and their friends gathered to roll balls down the alley and rejoice in each other's scores. Fun was their goal, friendship was their aim. Their existence was now, no past, no future, just the now.

George picked up Maggie on Saturday afternoon and they spent hours at the local soda shop which had a checkered floor, stools in front of the counter and slid into a brightly colored booth. They drank vanilla cokes and fed the juke box until their money ran out. They held hands, teased each other about bowling scores and which teachers they liked and which teachers they didn't like and discussed college applications which George had begun.

They watched *American Bandstand* at Maggie's house every week. After dusk they parked at the local teenage hangout overlooking a lake and kissed until they were saturated. Occasionally George would reach under Maggie's jacket and sweater and touch her bare skin which was enticing.

One weekend George asked her if she would like to go to a drive-in movie. She hesitated as she heard the rumors of couples going into the back seat and doing things she could only imagine.

"It might be cold in December," Maggie said wanting and not wanting to go.

"My dad's car has a heater and we can turn it on at intermission," George said.

"Okay, I'll ask my mother," Maggie said.

George pulled into the drive in, paid the cashier and found a spot in the middle row half way back from the screen. He placed the speaker on the window, adjusted it and rolled the window back up. Maggie slid across the front seat next to George. He kissed her cheek and they waited for the main feature *Love Me Tender* to come on the screen. At intermission George suggested they sit in the back seat. Maggie agreed although she knew she shouldn't. They'd been kissing more and more lately and it had been getting harder to stop. They settled in the back seat and George grasped her face and kissed her. She loved the way he kissed and loved the sensations aroused in her when he did. Maggie didn't give one thought to stopping him even when he reached under her skirt and unzipped his pants. Even when they did the irrevocable. She felt an awakening inside her that made it the right thing to do. She'd never felt anything so powerful: the comingling of bodies, the intimacy of touch, and the sensuous kisses. Saying no was impossible.

Maggie's eyes were fixed on the clock on the classroom wall. There were four minutes left until dismissal. She wondered if she could hold off the violent gag that lurched in her stomach. The bell rang and she flew into the corridor toward the bathroom covering her mouth. She made it inside the stall where she dropped her books and notepads on the floor and heaved into the toilet. A cold sweat crept over her and she thought she might pass out. She wiped her mouth with toilet paper and steadied herself as she watched a hand gather up her belongings that were strewn about. She turned and opened the door. Karen held out her hand and said, "C'mon, the bus leaves in five minutes." Karen wrapped Maggie's jacket around her and they headed out into the rawness of a February day.

Maggie wiped her eyes on the sleeve of her blouse and gazed around her bedroom. A poster of a swing dancer with a poodle skirt and saddle shoes was taped onto a wall between two windows. On her bureau pictures of her friends and her boyfriend, George, sat looking out at her. Her desk was littered with papers. George's school sweater imprinted with the letter B was draped over the chair. The lamp on her nightstand was covered with a ruffled blue shade; next to the lamp were her white AM radio and a hand held mirror.

She lifted her head, stood and picked up the mirror and for one brief moment caught a glimpse of her blue eyes, once radiant, now dull and puffy and honey colored hair that was askew. She managed to walk to the bathroom and repeatedly splashed cold water on her face trying to pack down the panic-stricken feeling she carried with her.

The crying stopped but the fear lingered. Her mind ran down all the possibilities: her father would never speak to her again, her mother would be heartbroken, and her brother would be to ashamed to be seen with her at school and even her friends might distance themselves from her.

How will I tell my parents? What will they do? What will happen to me? Pregnant and I have another year of high school. She patted her face with a towel, ran a comb through her hair, wrapped it in a ponytail and tucked her blouse into her skirt.

On the way back she passed her brother's bedroom. His door was closed. She heard the music of Chuck Berry coming from his hi-fi.

I hope he doesn't hate me. I hope he will not be embarrassed. I am so ashamed. I let my family down. What will they do? How will I tell them?

Maggie's mother and father were having their Friday night cocktails before dinner in the living room. Maggie paused at the top of the stairs listening quietly when she heard her father voice.

"Where's Mairead?" He was the only one to call her by her given name.

"Upstairs in her room. She looks a little pale lately but says she's alright. She seems grumpy, not her usual high spirited self. Goes right to her room every day after school instead of coming into the kitchen for an after school snack like she usually does," said her mother.

"It's those drive in movies she goes to with that Cooper fellow. I think we should stop that. They're nothing but passion pits. Teenagers have too much freedom nowadays. We need to slow things down. All this rock and roll music is everywhere. Gives them ideas," Henry said running his hand over his thinning gray hair as he flicked the ash from his cigarette into a large glass ashtray and took a sip of his drink.

"All the teenagers go there and George is a nice boy. I'm afraid the music is here to stay especially with this new singer, Elvis Presley."

"Is that the guy with the hips?" asked Henry.

"Yes."

"Things are happening too fast. I can feel change coming. I feel them pushing away from us and our way of living. She's out until 11 o'clock on Saturday night. Sometimes she and Ethan hurry through supper so they can listen to their records or call their friends on the phone. It didn't used to be that way. What is happening to our way of life? By the way, where is Ethan?"

"Upstairs listening to his hi fi. I asked him to keep his door closed to tone down the sound. He's happy he made the basketball team. He grew so much over the fall I'm sure the coach noticed. Don't worry, Henry, Maggie and Ethan have never given us anything to worry about. Maybe things are changing but they're fine."

Joan lay her knitting down and walked into the kitchen. She opened the oven door and basted the pieces of chicken. The kitchen table was set for four people. She removed two bottles of milk from the refrigerator and placed them on the table. Fine lines had started to appear around her eyes and streaks of white threaded their way through her sandy colored hair held back on one side with a barrette. She checked on the vegetables and returned to Henry.

Maggie retreated to her room and softly closed the door. *Maybe I should tell them now. Go right downstairs and say— Sorry about all the plans for college and a vacation to Maine this summer. I guess that can wait.*

She threw herself across her bed. Supper was in fifteen minutes.

———

A time of innocence and simplicity prevailed in the 1950s. The personal memories of WWll and stories of the great depression influenced young men to search for a smooth and secure future which they found in the availability of jobs coupled with marriage and parenthood. Families, such as the Porters, left the cities to live in subdivisions where housing was cheaper and close enough to the cities for work and shopping. American manufacturing switched from making war-related items to the automobile industry. There was a car in every driveway, a weekly paycheck and, after paying bills, there was some left over for savings. There were no credit cards. People borrowed money for a house and a car. Offices were closed Saturday and Sunday and retail shops closed Saturday at mid-day which was a social benefit for families wishing to spend time together. This was the Porters' way of life.

The Porters lived in a two story colonial with a center hall and stairs leading to the second floor bedrooms, a hallway lead to the kitchen in the back of the house. A living room was off to the left and a dining room was off to the right. The Porter family moved together in unity; dined together, went on outings together, met and chatted with their neighbors, and went to church every Sunday, all of which created peace and harmony in their lives. School was orderly; students dressed appropriately, stood during assembly and paid attention to the announcements. The Porters had one black and white television which they watched together and one dial telephone which hung on a wall in the kitchen. Henry Porter worked nine to five Monday through Friday; Joan did the household chores, cooked the meals and cared for the children. Maggie and Ethan respected their parents, did as they were told and referred to their neighbors as Mr. and Mrs. Sex was a taboo subject, there was no place for it. Sex outside of marriage was not acceptable and if a girl found herself "in the family way" she was shipped off to live with relatives or sent to a school for pregnant unmarried girls. The Porters knew no such girls.

———

The morning sickness continued with a vengeance at any time of the day, Maggie wondered why it was called that. *Am I being punished? Punished for getting pregnant* and *punished for doing this to my parents*.

Karen called Maggie every day after school and they spent part or whole of every weekend together.

One Saturday afternoon Karen and Maggie were at the soda shop. Karen sipped her vanilla coke. Maggie sat across from her wrapping a napkin around her fingers. "I'm so tired, Karen. I want to sleep all the time and yet I can't. Mom is going to notice."

"Come to my house for a sleepover and we can go to my room early. That way you can sleep all you want. Have you told George?"

"No. All he thinks about is basketball and college. How will I go to college? I can't even apply until the baby is born. I'm afraid of what will happen to me but more afraid of what will happen to the baby."

"I've heard about homes that girls go to have their babies."

"I can't leave home, Karen. To just go away from everything I know. I just can't."

"Maybe your mother will come up with something. Are you still throwing up? It must be awful."

"For the first time this morning I didn't. It's just the tiredness now."

"I don't think I'll ever get pregnant after seeing what happens."

"I guess it's okay if you're married and older. Like twenty one."

"When do you think the baby will be born?"

"My guess is September. I have five and a half months left. I popped a button on my cheerleading skirt doing some jumps. Scared me half to death because it made me realize I have to tell my parents and soon. My skirts are a little tight but I wear my blouses hanging out instead of tucked in."

"I'll wear mine hanging out too."

"Thanks, Karen. If I have to go away it will be the worst thing." Maggie fingered the four-leaf clover hanging around her neck. "Do you think I should tell George?"

"He's the father, of course you should tell him."

"It will be easier than telling my parents."

"Tell him and then tell your parents. It has to be done. You can't hide it forever. You're so tiny and it will start to show."

They left the soda shop together and rode their bikes home.

"Maggie, Ethan, supper," Joan called.

The family gathered around the table. Ethan packed his plate with food.

"Looks good, Mom," he said.

When the food was passed to Maggie she took small portions and moved them around on her plate.

13

"You better eat to stay in shape for cheerleading, Sis. I like having you cheer me on."

"Is that all you can think about? Basketball?" Maggie asked.

"Yeah." Ethan continued to clean his plate.

"Maggie, perhaps we could write to get some information about colleges you may be interested in. Do you have any idea where you would like to go? You shouldn't have any trouble getting in your marks are excellent and the teachers will give you good references..."

"Daddy, it's only the beginning of April, beside I don't know where I want to go. I'm going to my room," she announced and left the kitchen.

Maggie's father shrugged, her mother frowned, and Ethan's mouth hung open.

That evening when the family gathered to watch television, Maggie was absent, the only things on her mind was to call George and arrange to meet him the next morning to tell him her news.

Maggie sat in the booth at the soda shop waiting. George arrived and sat across from her.

"What gives?" he asked as he leaned toward Maggie.

"I think I'm pregnant."

George pulled back as if he had been hit with a baseball bat.

"Are you sure? I mean..."

"Yes, I am."

George reached for her hand. "Are you alright, I mean..."

"I throw up a lot and I am tired but the worst thing is what is going to happen. What should we do George? I'm so scared."

"I don't know. I'm going to college. My father will be furious if I don't go."

"But what about me? And what about the baby?"

"I'm so sorry. I didn't mean this to happen. I love you, Maggie."

Maggie lowered her eyes. "I love you, too, but this is a mess and I don't see how we can get out of it. I don't even know how to begin to tell them. I can't hide it much longer. And my brother will be so embarrassed."

"We could get married, you can finish school and I'll start college."

"There are no married girls at school and I don't know about the marriage thing. I'm sixteen you're eighteen. I can't even cook. Where would we live?"

"Being unmarried with a baby---it's just not right."

"My parents will ask me who the father is. I've got to tell them."

George dropped his head in his hands threading his fingers through his dark brown crew cut; weights of worry penetrated his mind: college, Maggie and their baby.

The enormity of the situation Maggie found herself in came crashing over her like melting icebergs sending torrent torpedoes to bodies of water that were ill equipped to handle it. Maggie remained silent her gaze wandering around her surroundings; kids from the neighborhood in another booth laughing and carrying on, families with young children eating ice cream while their mother dutifully wiped their messy chins.

"George, it has to be this weekend. I want to do it before anyone notices."

"What do think will happen?"

"I don't know. Maybe I could go away and leave the baby there and bring it home when I finish school. Maybe..." Maggie knew this would be impossible but she was clinging to the last thread of hope to keep her from falling apart.

"I have to have the car home by noon and," George said looking at his watch, "it's 11:30 now."

"Well, I don't know what will happen and what they will make me do but I will tell them this weekend and you better do the same."

Maggie and George left the soda shop and he drove Maggie home. Maggie got out of the car and said goodbye to handsome George.

Chapter Two

❧

Maggie entered the house and walked into the kitchen where her mother was taking brownies out of the oven; Maggie sat at the dinette set and watched her perform this task with grace. Her mother's early training as a dancer left her with a lithe body even into middle age. Maggie hoped she would have, at the very least, the gentleness and dignity her mother had naturally. Maggie loved sitting in the kitchen with her mother nibbling on brownies, warm from the oven. The canary yellow kitchen cabinets and white valance over the kitchen window lifted Maggie's spirit most days but not today. Her mother turned, brushing a thread of hair from her cheek. "Hello, Maggie. I didn't hear you come in. How was your morning with George?"

"Okay."

"I'm going to have a slice of toast would you like some?"

"Yes, please."

Her mother placed two slices in the toaster and retrieved strawberry jam from the refrigerator. Sunshine seeped through the kitchen window over the sink casting a glow across the linoleum floor.

Maggie watched her mother whose movements were smooth and unhurried. The toast popped up and when the smearing of jam was complete, Joan turned toward Maggie, who was crying silently. "Maggie, what is...?"

"Mom, I think I'm pregnant." Tears turned into sobs. Joan dropped the plate which crashed into tiny pieces as the toast scattered onto the floor.

"Maggie, it can't be, you're only sixteen. You're still in high school. How did this happen? Are you sure?" Joan stepped over the broken pieces her eyes wide, her lips parted and sat next to Maggie at the table.

"Tell me it isn't so. There must be some mistake!"

Maggie moved her head from side to side.

"Are you alright, I mean are you sick? You're only sixteen," she repeated, as she reached over the table to touch her daughter."

"I'm okay mom, but what am I going to do?"

"How far along...when did you know...is it George Cooper?" The questions tumbled out of her mother's mouth.

"I've missed three periods. Yes, George is the father."

Joan stood and paced around the kitchen. "Do his parents know? He's going to college. My God, what is in store for you? How will we do this?"

"George is telling his parents this weekend. How should we tell Daddy? And what about Ethan?"

"Daddy is out getting tires for his car and picking Ethan up after basketball practice. We will tell them when they come home. Yes, that is what we will do." She stopped pacing and faced Maggie. "Does anyone else know?"

"Only George and he is telling his parents this weekend and Karen."

"Karen knows!"

"Yes, she sort of figured it out."

Joan's mind raced forward. *How will we stem the tide of this secret from flowing further? No one else must know. A litany of sto-*

ries would be made up: go away to a relative, boarding school, has to be soon. But, the baby. The baby...

"Mom?"

"Yes dear," Joan answered as she recovered.

"What's going to happen, Mom? I'm scared. I can't go back to school. What will I do?"

Joan sat down across from Maggie and covered her daughter's hands with her own. "Don't worry, we will think of something," Joan said, her green eyes tearing as she spoke.

Maggie and her mother cleaned up the broken pieces and tossed the toast into the garbage. They walked from the kitchen through the dining room across the hall to the living room where they sat and began their wait for Henry and Ethan to arrive.

Maggie heard her father's car pull into the driveway. She jumped up, "Mom, I'm shaking."

"You have to tell them."

Ethan came into the kitchen first and spotted the brownies. He cut a square and ate it in one gulp.

"Ethan," Joan called, "we're in here."

"What's going on? Maggie you look white."

"Sit down, Ethan." Joan said.

Henry entered the house through the kitchen, closed the door and hung up his jacket.

Maggie stood in back of the sofa kneading the back of it with her sweaty palms. Her heart was racing and tiny beads of moisture broke out over her upper lip. If only she could run away and not have to face what she had to do. She heard her father's footsteps approaching the living room.

"Well what do we owe this to? Everyone's here," said Henry.

Joan stood up and held onto the arm of the wing back chair.

"Maggie has something to tell you," Joan said and turned toward Maggie.

Henry looked at Maggie and waited. At first she could not speak. She cleared her throat and then blurted out her news.

"What! What did you say?" Her father asked.

"I think I'm pregnant. I'm so sorry. We didn't mean for this to happen."

Her father's six foot frame swayed as he lost his equilibrium momentarily. Silence cast a pall over the family. It was broken by Ethan who said. "But you're not married."

Henry managed to reach a chair and lower himself into it.

"That's this guy George's fault. It's him, isn't it? Isn't it?"

"Yes, but__" she didn't finish.

"I knew it, I knew it! Where have I been?" He stood throwing his hands up in the air.

Her mother waited silently.

"That's all that guy was here for. If I'd known I would've rung his neck. Are you sure of this?"

"Yes."

"How long have you known?"

"Three months.

"And does he know?"

"Yes."

"And what does he intend to do?"

"He did mention marriage."

"How would he support you?"

Maggie shrugged her shoulders.

"Marriage is out of the question. You can't support a baby. You're both too young. No one can find out about this. We'll be disgraced. You've got to finish high school one way or another."

"Henry," Joan interjected, "there's a private girl's school in the next town. She can go there."

"Do they take pregnant sixteen year olds? I think not."

"Can't she just stay here with us?" asked Ethan.

"And what? Live inside the house for six months," said Henry. "Out of the question. School is over for you, Mairead. We'll get a tutor for now. Joan get her to a doctor out of town to see if this is true."

"School is over for me. But__"

"But what?" her father asked.

"What about the baby?"

"You can't keep it. It will be a disgrace for us and the baby."

"But what will I do?"

"Give it up for adoption, of course. It will have a mother and a father. An illegitimate baby will have a hard time in life. Now, stop your crying, Mairead. You've gotten yourself into a big mess and we have to get you out of it. I'm sure we can find a place for you to go."

"Go?" Maggie wailed. "Where will I go?"

"Henry," his wife pleaded, "she can__"

"She can what, Joan? Stay here for everyone to see? No! She goes away and gives the baby up for adoption."

"But how will we know who's taking it?" asked Ethan.

"They have people checking into these things," said Henry.

"Adoption. But... but... just like that? I'll leave school, but can't I keep the baby?" Maggie stammered. The words "goes away—adoption" exploded in her head. She covered her ears.

"Absolutely not. What do you know about babies?"

"Mom can help me. Can't you, Mom?"

"Oh, Maggie." Joan reached out for her daughter.

Maggie stood up and in a clear voice said. "This is my baby I want to keep it."

Henry took three strides across the room and came face to face with Maggie who did not shrink back and in a loud clear voice said, "You listen to me. You will do exactly as you are told; you'll stay out of school, go to a doctor, and if you are pregnant, you will go away to have the baby and give it up for adoption. End of story. No one must find out about this. You've shamed us! Do you understand? Do you?"

"Yes." a tear spilled over Maggie's flushed cheeks.

Her father went outside to the back yard. Maggie heard him moan out loud. "Mairead, Mairead."

Joan got out of her chair, walked over to Maggie and put her arms around her, stroking her hair, their combined tears mingled on their cheeks. "Shh, shh," she soothed, rocking her gently.

Ethan approached them and laid his hand on Maggie's arm. "I'm sorry, Maggie. It'll be alright, you'll see."

Maggie looked at him through blurred eyes, released herself from her mother and went to her room where she stayed for the rest of the day refusing to speak to anyone. She left the tray her mother brought to her untouched.

The next morning Henry called the Coopers. Frank answered.

"Hello."

"Is this Frank Cooper?"

"Yes, it is."

"This is Henry Porter. Your son and my daughter have been seeing a lot of each other."

"Yes, I know. Is anything wrong?"

"Plenty. Maggie thinks she's pregnant. Got that? And your son is the father. You tell him to keep away from my daughter. He's done enough damage. If he shows up here I'll have him arrested!" Henry slammed the phone down.

Frank Cooper held the receiver in his hand. "Oh my God!" he said out loud. His wife, Rita, joined him.

"What is it?" she asked.

"That girl George has been seeing says she's pregnant."

Frank and Rita sat in their living room digesting the news. They stared at each other in disbelief. Were the plans they had for their only son shattered?

"What about college?" asked Rita.

Frank stood. "Let's see about this."

"George, George! Are you up there?" his father called

"Yes. What's up?"

"Come down here immediately," his father ordered.

George heard the phone ring and heard his parent's loud voices. His stomach clenched as he headed downstairs to face his parents. His mother was leaning over the kitchen table one hand covering her mouth. His father stood with his feet apart, hands on his hips.

"What's up with that Porter girl? Her father just called."

"I was going to tell you__"

"When? Just when were you going to tell us? When she shows up at our door with a baby? We don't even know those people. How do you know it's yours?"

"Dad, it's mine."

"Look, you're going to college and nothing is going to get in the way of that. Do you understand?"

"Yes. What will she do?"

"That's not our concern," Frank shot back.

"We could get married."

"Married! You must be joking. You're eighteen years old and on your way to college. You get married and your life is over. How would you support a family? By working as a bagger in a grocery store? Where will you live? Out of the question. You think I want this whole town to know you got a girl pregnant?"

"But if it's George's baby, it's our grandchild," said Rita.

"You can stop thinking like that right now," ordered Frank. He turned to his son.

"How could you have been so stupid, George?"

"I don't know. We never thought this would happen."

"You've got to stay away from her. Don't even speak to her at school."

George winced at his father's demand.

Chapter Three

❧

It was a rainy April day, with gusts swirling among the trees bending branches but not breaking them. Maggie had slept late putting off the inevitable doctor's appointment scheduled for one o'clock that afternoon. Her mother's usual calm manner was replaced by useless chatter and did nothing to relieve the tension present in the car during the trip to the office.

Maggie kept her trembling hands folded in her lap as she and her mother sat in the waiting room. There were six chairs, four of them unoccupied. Magazines with pictures on the covers of pregnant women, all smiles, hands wrapped around their protruding abdomens were stacked on an end table. There were pictures of newborns snuggled in their mother's arms. Maggie's throat constricted.

The door to the inner office opened and a tall thin nurse with a compressed smile appeared. She was dressed in white: white stockings, white shoes and a white stiff uniform in keeping with the expression on her face. She glanced at the papers in her hand and called Maggie's name. Maggie could not respond. Rising slowly, her mother acknowledged the nurse with a nod. Maggie stood and followed behind the nurse and her mother.

Maggie sat on the examining room table wearing only a flimsy gown with a thin sheet covering her. She felt stripped of her dignity as she crossed her ankles and closed her eyes. Thoughts of her friend, Karen and George crept into her mind; the proms were approaching. Would Billy Walsh ask Karen? Would George ask someone? She feared her heart would break if he did. The months of building her world around George peeled away leaving raw, ragged wounds.

Maggie realized her days of innocence were slipping away. She would give birth to a human being, part of her whom she might never see.

A man of average height with close cropped white hair, wearing a white coat and oval wire-rimmed glasses walked in. He spoke with authority, the stiff nurse stood by in silence.

"What seems to be the problem?" asked Dr. Jones.

"My daughter thinks she might be pregnant."

"Why do you think that?" he asked, addressing Maggie.

"I haven't had a period since December and I can't button my skirt."

"Well, it all fits. Lay back on the table and we'll find out," he requested as he placed the folder on a table and put on a pair of gloves.

When he finished the examination he removed the gloves, placed them in a sink, and told Maggie she could sit up.

"You're in your fourth month. Do you plan on getting married?"

Tears sprung blurring her vision but she responded to his question by shaking her head.

"What do you intend to do?"

Maggie couldn't answer, she felt embarrassed and cheated but most of all she felt remorse for her baby. Her chin quivered, she squeezed her eyes shut and tears flowed from the corners. Dr. Jones offered no solace. His eyes shifted to Joan, who answered for Maggie.

"Give the baby up for adoption."

Maggie stifled a scream. She swallowed quickly and both hands went to the four-leaf clover around her neck.

"There are homes that she can go to until the baby is born. They are specifically for unmarried young women who are going to give up their babies for adoption. They will take care of everything for you. I'll have my secretary give you information about them," said the doctor.

Maggie dressed, her thinness had given way to a thickened waist and her bra was uncomfortable even on the first hook. On the way out the receptionist handed her some pamphlets that she looked at indifferently. It all sounded so uncaring, just go away and give the baby up for adoption, her baby, George's baby. Not one person asked how she felt. Her jaw tightened, faces appeared in her mind: handsome George, sympathetic Ethan, smiling Karen, her sad mother, her angry father. She struggled with the images waiting for them to disappear.

Climbing into the car Maggie tossed the pamphlets onto the dashboard and ignored them as they slid off when her mother turned the corner into their street. Maggie entered the house through the kitchen and ran her hand over her mother's white apron with daisies around the edges. She continued into the dining room, remembering the birthdays, anniversaries and holiday dinners that were held there. Maggie felt a shift from a stable and predictable life to an uncertain one in uncharted waters. New paint or wallpaper would not cover up the secret that was buried in the house; it would remain buried and unspoken about.

Maggie trudged up to her room and laid face down on her bed shielding her eyes from all the familiarity of her room which she would leave to live with strangers in a strange place. These thoughts made her weep, weep for her old life, weep for her baby, and weep for herself.

There was a soft knock on the door

"Would you like something to eat, Maggie?" asked her mother.

Maggie looked at her mother with pleading eyes. "No, Mom. How long can I stay home?"

"Let's not talk about it right now__"

"When should we talk about it, Mom?"

Joan sat down on the edge of the bed across from Maggie laced her fingers together and blinked several times before she spoke.

"The first thing is getting you a tutor so that your school work will not be interrupted. I will contact your teacher to tell her you will not be returning to school."

"What will you tell her?"

"Most people know Uncle Bob in Florida had a stroke and Aunt Clara cares for him. We will say you are going down there to help her and she specifically asked if you could come."

More lies more secrets.

Pangs of fear and remorse pierced Maggie's thoughts; how proud her parents were of her, teachers raved about her class-room ability and friends flocked around her. It would take years to redeem herself in their eyes. It would hang over her like a rain cloud releasing drops of anguish whenever she thought she had paid her dues.

Joan patted Maggie's arm and stood. "I'm going downstairs, come when you're ready."

Joan sat in the living room knitting, pulling yarn from the basket, working the needles to create new stiches and keep the yarn from unraveling. She had no idea what the finished product would be only that she had to knit. The back door opened and Ethan called. "Mom."

"Here, Ethan, in the living room." Ethan's height filled a room. He tossed his books on the couch, sat down and asked his mother where Maggie was. Joan removed her glasses and looked up at her son with hair the color of nutmeg that never laid flat. Ethan sat down.

"In her room. We just came back from the doctor, it's true." Joan choked on the words. "Maggie's pregnant."

Ethan bowed his head. He felt embarrassed, ashamed and afraid for his sister and his family. When he looked up he saw his mother's moistened eyes brimming with tears. His mother wiped other people's tears, now she had her own.

"Kids at school are asking where she is, I told them she was sick."

"That's fine. We'll figure all that out tonight when Daddy comes home."

Joan was still knitting the unidentifiable object when Henry came home. He didn't remove his coat he went directly to the living room where Maggie and Ethan sat watching their mother working the knitting needles. Henry stood rigid as if someone called ATTENTION! He knew at that moment the very foundation of everything they stood for and believed in had been shaken loose.

"Daddy," Maggie began, "I am so sorry."

"Yes, we all are, but now we must make plans before the fabric of our family is completely torn away. No one must know about this, our reputation as a family must be preserved especially Mairead's. The baby must be given to a family, a mother and a father and not grow up with the stigma of illegitimacy."

"Kids are asking at school where Maggie is," said Ethan.

Momentary silence came over the family when a loud thump on the front door was heard followed by yelling. "Maggie, Maggie..."

Maggie leapt to the door but was intercepted by her father.

"I'll handle this."

Henry opened the front door and saw a distraught George, his hair uncombed, his hands on his hips. "I want to see Maggie."

Henry was about to close the door and George put his foot in the doorway preventing this from happening giving Maggie just enough time to run out the side door and meet George on the front lawn. Joan reached Henry's side, held his arm and said, "Let them be."

Henry watched at the opened door as Maggie and George stood on the lawn, holding hands. Maggie bent her head and listened as George spoke to her in a low voice. George kissed Maggie and she waited until he drove away. Going back into the house she passed her father and joined her mother and Ethan in the living room. Henry closed the door, removed his coat, loosened his tie and joined his family, his face ashen.

Joan explained to Henry about Uncle Bob. Maggie felt like a silent partner in a conspiracy as she watched the players recite their lines each with their own emphasis on words such as secret, tutor, go away, hide, must not be seen. The word baby was never uttered. The chatter of these voices around her; her father's deep resonant voice, her mother's soft voice and Ethan's high pitched voice were dimmed. Her father paced, her mother sat on the edge of her seat, and Ethan stood arms folded.

Maggie shouted. "Please stop!"

The voices became silent, all heads turned toward Maggie. She stood straight, her head held high with her feet planted firmly on the floor, arms at her side and began. "I will not have a tutor. I have two months left of my junior year. I have all A's. I'm sure if I keep up with homework and pass the exams I can complete the year. It's only two months. Karen will bring the homework and pass it in for me."

"But__" Joan said.

"Karen can be trusted. This is all I am asking. Mom, you can tell the teacher I came down with an illness that requires me to stay home. I can have secrets and lies too." Maggie halted for a second and headed to the kitchen to dial Karen's number and put her plan into place.

Maggie went to her bedroom followed by Ethan. She sat on the side of her bed and Ethan sat cross legged on the floor. She listened as her parents' voices rose from the living room getting louder and louder until she got up and closed her bedroom door.

"What do you want me to do?" asked Ethan.

"Nothing, just be my brother."

Too embarrassed to go out, Maggie spent most days in her room reading. She ate after her parents were finished; she watched television when her parents were busy doing other things. When her mother approached her she would listen and nod and continue reading *Gone with the Wind* for the second time. Her father and she ignored each other and spoke only on rare occasions. She wrote letters to George and tore them into bits.

One evening Maggie was watching television and suddenly she felt something stir inside of her. She waited. There it was again, a soft fluttering feeling. Her mind shifted. There was a baby growing inside of her. A new life, one in which she would have no role.

Karen arrived Tuesdays and Thursdays with an armful of homework and a litany of school gossip. Karen's mother dropped her off and Maggie's mother drove her home. Neither mother discussed with each other the circumstances of Maggie's home confinement; they supported their daughters' plan and made every effort to help with it.

Karen buoyed Maggie's spirits which had been dampened for so long. On various occasions Karen would bring new pony tail holders, a hot fudge sundae, the latest copy of *16* and on her last visit brought her a brown teddy bear with a red ribbon wrapped around its neck.

Karen's brown curls were frizzled from the June humidity but her brown eyes sparkled and her animated stories distracted the sadness during their last visit together.

"Take him with you when you go, maybe you can leave it for the baby. I wish I could come visit you."

"Me too," said Maggie. "Only Ethan and Mom will come."

"Promise me you won't be sad when I leave."

"I am sure I will be but you have done so much for me without you it would have been unbearable."

"I'll be thinking of you. Ethan will fill me in. Maggie, I think George must know I come to see you. He asked me to tell you he was thinking of you."

Maggie's heart beat a little faster. She ran her hands over her thighs, swallowed hard and said, "Tell him I said hi."

"I will." Karen turned and left Maggie's room before she would release her tears.

Joan had located a place and as soon as Maggie finished school they packed the car in preparation to leave the following day. Henry left for work early to avoid saying goodbye to Maggie; Ethan hugged his sister promising to see her soon. Maggie sat beside her mother as the car pulled out of the driveway and Ethan stood waving to them from the front window.

Trying to avoid the pot holes, Maggie's mother swerved around a tree lined driveway leading up to Swan Point Home where Maggie would spend the last three months of her pregnancy. Noticing the swans swimming in the pond, Maggie rolled down the window to see a family gliding by. A signet was perched on the back of one of them. They appeared attached. She watched until she could no longer see the swan family and as she sat back in her seat saw a looming structure ahead. The first thing Maggie noticed was bars on the curtain less windows on the second and third floor. A shiver ran through her. The building was three stories high built of stone, the windows were untrimmed and there were several nondescript bushes in front of the building, a pillar on each side of the top step led to a massive front door with a rusted door knocker. The man mowing the expansive lawn did not look up as the car approached. Maggie and her mother got out of the car and headed up the steps which fanned out at the bottom and narrowed at the top. Chairs and rockers were scattered about the front porch all unoccupied. They knocked on the door and waited. A pregnant girl answered and Maggie's grip on her suitcase tightened.

"Hi, come on in, my name is Donna. Have a seat here," she said pointing to chairs lined up against the wall. "I'll get Mrs. Chase for you." Her stomach protruded in front of her accentuating her skinny arms and legs. Her straight brown hair hung loose around her face as she lowered her big brown eyes to give a quick look at Maggie's body.

Maggie leaned back. *I can't do this. I want to go home where I belong.* Her mother took her hand, Maggie grasped it and took a step into the foyer in which dark wood paneling covered the walls, wooden floors creaked beneath her feet and a musty smell permeated the air. Maggie sat on the edge of a chair clutching her suitcase.

Within minutes Mrs. Chase appeared her footsteps light and quick. She was two inches taller than Maggie and wore her gray hair piled on top of her head. She had a broad smile on her face that gave the impression of being permanent. Maggie looked into Mrs. Chase's nearly black eyes. They seemed to drill into hers. Mrs. Chase grabbed Maggie's hand. Maggie could not tell if the woman was welcoming her or challenging her. Letting her own hand go limp, Maggie withdrew first.

"I'm Mrs. Chase, you must be Maggie and you must be her mother. Come with me."

Mrs. Chase led them down a long hallway. Three pregnant girls passed them on their way, two looked straight ahead; one of them gave Maggie a closed mouth smile. Mrs. Chase unlocked the door of her office and asked them to be seated.

"Now," she began scribbling in her notebook, "how far along are you Maggie?"

"Six months," said Maggie and burst into tears. Joan sprang to her daughter's rescue and held her head close to her. "It's okay, honey, it's okay," murmured Joan. Mrs. Chase sat by quietly, listening and waiting.

Six months and I have three to go. I have to live with complete strangers for three months. And then what? No baby. Who will I leave my baby with? How will I get along here? How could my parents do this to me and my baby?"

Maggie blew her nose and let out a heavy sigh. Joan loosened her grip and pulled her chair next to Maggie's.

"Now then," Mrs. Chase continued, "beside your mother who do you want to visit you here?"

"My brother, Ethan."

"How about your father?'

Her mother started to answer but Mrs. Chase held up her hand and looked at Maggie.

"He's not coming and I don't want him here. Says I disgraced the family and he's afraid people will find out."

"She doesn't mean that," her mother interjected.

"That's usual, but he may change his mind and you may change yours. How about the father of the baby?"

"No." Maggie murmured.

"Okay. Now, we have excellent teachers here. We have class during the summer months. Each girl is assigned chores that she will be expected to carry out. Your visitors can come anytime except during school hours which are nine o'clock in the morning to three o'clock in the afternoon. You will be assigned a social worker. In your case it is Ann Marie Hale. We do not use last names for our girls here for privacy reasons and if you want to be known as other than Maggie you can tell me now and I will introduce you with that name."

"My name is Maggie."

"Fine. You also will have regular checkups with our doctors. Now then, is there anything else?" she asked as she closed her notebook shut.

Nothing else, except who will take my baby and I don't know anybody here.

Mrs. Chase went on, "Here at Swan Point we realize this is a very difficult situation for you but I can assure you we will do our best to help you through it. We have young women from all walks of life and from varied backgrounds. Some have limited family resources and some have an abundance of family resources but here we treat everyone the same. We have a reputation of being a place that is safe and we take good care of our girls. Now, come, let me show you to your room."

Mrs. Chase led them up the wide staircase. At the landing, Maggie saw an enormous painting of an elderly gentleman sitting in an arm chair, his white beard almost obscuring his face. Next to him stood a lovely older woman in a long dress with ruffled sleeves that ended at her wrist. Her sad face and sad eyes caused Maggie to stop and stare.

"That is Mr. and Mrs. Worthington. They were our sponsors and donated this building to us for unmarried pregnant teenagers. They spent weekends here until their fourteen year old daughter became pregnant, ran away and was never heard from again," said Mrs. Chase. Maggie's chin dropped.

They continued up the next flight to a long dark hallway. Large numbers were attached on the outside of each door. They arrived at number 208. Mrs. Chase opened the unlocked door, walked in and opened a window as wide as she could to let a slight breeze into the bedroom through the bars. The room had two single metal beds each covered with a faded chenille bedspread with a nightstand in between. On the nightstand was a small lamp, a clock and some paperback books. One bed had some clothes strewn about on it, some were unevenly folded. Shoes and slippers were sticking out from underneath it. Mrs. Chase pointed at the empty bed.

"That one is yours, Maggie. We do not allow personal items from home like posters, stuffed animals or spreads due to the fact that some girls may not have these items and some have more than enough. You may bring in notepads, writing paper but no novels. We have a small library and you can chose books from there. These are temporary quarters they are not dormitories. Sheets, pillow cases and towels are provided. Every Friday by seven o'clock you will leave your laundry outside the door in a marked laundry bag and it will be returned by three o'clock that day. The bureau is shared and the bathrooms are down the hall."

Maggie eyed the surroundings that would be her home for three months. The moss green bureau had a missing knob; the walls were painted white but had yellowed over time. She placed her suitcase on the bed, the mattress was unyielding. Maggie pushed the mattress down with her hand and it didn't budge, like a board, hard and stiff.

"Your roommate is Olivia. I believe she's outside at the moment. You must understand that in no circumstances will we tolerate unruly behavior or outbursts and you are expected to attend class and do your chores as assigned. Supper is at six o'clock and all visitors must leave at that time. Understood?"

"Yes."

"I'll leave you two to unpack. You will meet Ann Marie first thing in the morning after breakfast. You will be very busy here, Maggie. If you need to see me, just tell Ann Marie and she will arrange it. I live here on the third floor so I'm always around. That goes for you, too, Joan. You might be interested to know that I had to give up my baby for adoption but there was nothing like this. I was sent to live out of state with a grouchy aunt. Once I got over it, I planned to establish a place for unmarried girls. Sort

of like a home away from home. So you see good things sometimes come out of bad things." She turned, headed for the door
but stopped. "One last thing, Maggie. This experience will move
your heart. It will make your life matter."

Maggie sat on the bed, elbows on her knees, chin resting in
her hands. She was oblivious to her mother opening drawers,
checking closet space, unlatching luggage, adjusting the lamp,
and clock on the nightstand while moving about the room.

Joan opened the first two drawers of the bureau and when
she saw clothing she closed them immediately and finding the
lower two drawers empty placed Maggie's clothing in them; five
maternity tops, four skirts with gaping openings and a cloth tie
for the waist, underwear, socks and night wear, all of which had
been chosen by her because Maggie refused to shop for maternity
clothes.

"I hope the food is good and you get enough rest..." Joan's
words fell on deaf ears; she was cut off by a girl with a slightly
protruding belly entering the room. The girl sauntered over and
flung her books on the bed tossing her black hair away from her
face. Hands on her hips her eyes wide open she said in a clear
forceful voice.

"I hate this place and can't wait for it to be over."

Joan stopped unpacking, Maggie's eyebrows shot upward
and her mouth hung open.

The girl turned toward Maggie and said. "Welcome to the fun
house. You're lucky, my mother left me in the front hall said she
would be back when it was over. I'm Olivia. When are you due?"

"September, early September," Maggie said.

"Me too, late September. What's your name?"

"Maggie. This is my mother."

Olivia glanced at Joan and Joan nodded.

"The food is good, the social workers are a joke and everyone
says giving up the kid is a swell idea."

Maggie grabbed the unfamiliar chenille spread so unlike her smooth blue comforter in her bedroom at home. She swallowed hard to rid herself of the lump in her throat. There were no words forming in her mouth. Desperation set in, she unloosened her grip on the spread, dashed out of the room and down the stairs stopping at the massive door laying her hands on it and leaning her forehead on it. Just as she did this she saw a hand grasp the knob and turn it.

"Allow me. It can get stuffy in the rooms, maybe a little fresh air will help you sort things out," said Mrs. Chase as she opened the door. "Sit in one of the rocking chairs. I'll bring you some lemonade."

Maggie felt ashamed, embarrassed and helpless. She watched as several groups of girls in various stages of pregnancy sat on the lawn chatting amiably. She wondered if she would reach that stage and be able to adjust to her life at Swan Point Home for the next three months which seemed like forever to her. Were all the girls like Olivia? Did they hate it here?

Mrs. Chase came with a tall glass of lemonade. Maggie took a sip of the drink that had just enough sugar to avoid the tart taste of the lemons. She finished it off in one gulp.

"Feel better?"

"A little."

"It will take some time getting used to it here but after a bit you will be okay, you'll see."

Just then Joan and Olivia arrived and sat quietly next to Maggie.

"I don't know what happened, I just got scared," said Maggie.

"Mrs. Chase said I could come early tomorrow, so I will arrive first thing in the morning. Is there anything you want or need?"

Olivia looked on and then cast her eyes downward.

"Yes, brownies and bring enough for Olivia."

Joan glanced at Olivia. "Of course." She kissed Maggie on the cheek. "Goodbye. Goodbye Olivia. I'll see you both tomorrow." Joan hastened down the steps and did not look back, she just couldn't.

"That's some mother you got there," said Olivia. "C'mon, Maggie, It's six o'clock. Time for supper. You'll meet the rest of the outcasts."

Maggie followed four steps behind Olivia. Meals were eaten in a large dining room with windows overlooking the back yard and a view of the pond. A stack of trays stood at the entrance next to knives, forks and spoons in holders. Food was served by the kitchen staff with expressionless faces who spoke only in terms of food. Maggie entered the line in back of Olivia. She pushed her tray along staring at mashed potatoes, green beans, corn and meatloaf, none of which appealed to her.

Strange faces were everywhere most of which belonged to young girls in various stages of pregnancy. Maggie followed Olivia's every move. A plate of food appeared on the counter. Maggie placed it on her tray, drinks and dessert were at the end. Olivia led them to a large table that was half occupied. Maggie stuck to Olivia hoping she would get through the first night without bursting into tears.

"This is Maggie, just got here."

Maggie nodded to the girls around the table. There were no greetings just stares as they drank their milk and picked at their food. Maggie wanted to flee but she held on to the edge of her chair with both hands.

"Let go of the chair, Maggie. You'll need your hands to eat," whispered Olivia.

"Mom says I should eat so the baby will get adopted quicker," announced one of the girls slipping potatoes between her lips.

"My mom says, 'Just deliver the baby and you will forget about it afterward'."

"My mom said, 'Go live with your sister afterward because you can't come back here'."

"I don't know what my parents told the teachers or even what they told my sister about me leaving. They forbid me to say anything. It was all so secret. I wonder what they'll say when I come back. Have a nice vacation?"

"I will never make the same mistake again, falling for some boy. Look where it got me and he's off the hook. My mother comes to visit and she doesn't even ask how I am. I mean look at me, eight months pregnant and she ignores it."

"My dad is more worried about people finding out than he is about me."

Maggie placed her fork on her plate wiped her mouth and said. "That's the way my father felt. He said I disgraced the family. He never said goodbye to me when I left to come here."

"My mom hasn't been to see me in three weeks. She's probably too busy with her boyfriend. Wonder what she'd do if she knew the baby was his?"

"Where will you go when you get out?" asked Maggie.

"Maybe I'll just stay here. Maybe I'll kill myself."

Maggie eyebrows arched. Mrs. Chase appeared from nowhere, caressed the girl and walked her into the living area.

"Does anyone know how Jessica is?" asked one girl.

Olivia leaned over to Maggie. "Jessica is fourteen. Her father is a big shot doctor in Boston. Jessica was raped at a pool party her parents were having. Her mother never forgave her dad for having the party or Jessica for getting pregnant. Her dad sends a specialist to take care of her. He and an aunt take turns coming to see her. She was pretty sick, she's better now but still cries a lot."

Maggie's lips formed an O.

"There are a few kids here from rich families. One is the daughter of the former Mayor of New York, she's fifteen. And then there's me, with nothing and nobody. Here's Jessica now. Over here, Jessica," said Olivia.

Jessica lay her tray down on the table. Her face is pale, her cheeks sunken in which made her eyes look bigger than they actually were. Her limp black hair hung loose. There was sadness in her expression that was deep and seemed to penetrate her body. Her advanced pregnancy overwhelmed the rest of her.

"This is Maggie, got here today, Jessica," said Olivia. Jessica looked through Maggie. Maggie smiled and said, "Hi Jessica."

"Hi."

"I heard you were sick. Are you better now?" asked Maggie.

"Mm."

The stories had a common thread; secrecy and shame. Maggie's war with herself began to subside.

The girls shied away from revealing intimate details of family and the fathers of their babies but shared their feelings of guilt, shame, abandonment and fear. One by one girls would disappear and new arrivals would take their place. There were no goodbyes just hellos.

Olivia drank her milk and finished her supper. "C'mon Maggie. Let's go outside."

Maggie and Olivia sat on the grass overlooking the pond. Maggie sat cross legged. Olivia leaned back on one elbow.

"Are you going to finish high school?" asked Maggie.

"Fat chance of that. What will I tell everyone?"

"You could go to another school where no one knows you."

"Maybe."

"I'm going to finish and then go to college."

"College. I could never go. No money."

"There must be something you can do."

"I guess I'll finish high school and go from there."

"Good."

"Does the Father of your baby know where you are?' asked Maggie.

"Doesn't know I'm pregnant."

"You mean you didn't tell him?"

"Why should I? He'd blab it all over the place. Does the Father of your baby know?"

Maggie nodded.

"So, did you love this guy?" asked Olivia.

"I guess so. At least that's what it felt like. We had so much fun together."

"I had no one. My dad left when I was little and my mom worked two jobs to keep us afloat. I was left with babysitters and watched TV while they made out. This guy made me feel special. He wanted one thing. What a jerk."

My dad would never leave us and the only babysitter I had was my Irish grandmother.

"This will be over soon, Olivia, and when it is we've got to go on."

"Maybe it would be simpler not to think too much."

Caroline and Barbara joined Maggie and Olivia on the grass.

Caroline sprawled on the grass and gazed up at the sun.

"I have two weeks to go. Finally it will be over."

"I have three weeks to go. I wonder how graduation went and the prom..." said Barbara.

Olivia glared at Barbara.

"You're gonna have a baby and give it away and you're wondering about a prom?"

"Yes I am. I was supposed to be prom queen! My friends probably don't know what happened to me. One day I'm in school the next day I'm gone!"

Maggie spoke up.

"That's what happened to most of us. I thought I was the only one this happened to. At least we can talk to each other. I was told the baby needed a mother and a father who are married and being unmarried would make life hard for the baby but we are the Mothers."

"Hard for the baby but what about us?" asked Caroline

"Doesn't matter, we disappear and all is forgotten," said Olivia.

"My mom told me they would give me something during labor to help me forget everything," said Caroline.

The girls fell silent. A slice of their lives had been cut out. There was no joy only loneliness. Loneliness for past lives, loneliness for a soothing word. Life was painful and its pain was in the silence. They would listen to each other's stories and tend each other's wounds but in the end they would deliver their babies alone and return home to silence.

The sun was dipping behind the clouds and the four girls headed to the house. Maggie and Olivia undressed and slipped under the bed covers. Maggie felt a big bump on her lumpy pillow. She reached under and felt the brown teddy bear with the red ribbon which was comforting but her night was long and laborious as her baby moved inside her leaving her in a state of sleeplessness. How would she navigate through the waters of the next three months? Her meeting with Ann Marie Hale was the next morning.

The bell clanged at six thirty in the morning. Maggie sat bolt upright in bed.

"Easy, Maggie. Happens every morning. Get used to it," said Olivia.

Breakfast was in the same dining room. Maggie knew a few of the girls from the previous evening which was a comfort to her. After breakfast, Mrs. Chase called the new arrivals to a table set off to one side. There were several other people at the table. Maggie was the first called.

"Maggie, this is Ann Marie, your social worker. You will be with her for the entire morning."

Ann Marie had black hair that fell just to the top of her shoulders with bangs almost covering her dark eyes. She was short and wore red lipstick. Her black skirt fell just below her knees. A sleeveless white blouse buttoned to the top showed off her tanned arms. From her ears dangled the largest hoop earrings that Maggie had ever seen. She clutched a notebook close to her chest.

"Pleased to meet you, Maggie. Come with me."

Maggie followed Ann Marie's quick steps to an office on the first floor.

There was a worn wooden desk in the center of the room. After opening a window, Ann Marie took her place behind the desk and motioned Maggie to have a seat across from her. The look on Ann Marie's face was serious, not grim, but serious as if she had an important task to perform. Ann Marie brushed her bangs to one side and looked directly at Maggie. Maggie sensed kindness in her expression and her shoulders relaxed although she held on to the sides of her chair.

"How is everything so far Maggie?"

Maggie shrugged her shoulders. *I just got here.*

Ann Marie picked up a pen and opened the notebook. Inside was a folder and on the outside was written, Maggie September 1957.

"I see your given name is Mairead. That is a beautiful name."

"It's Irish for Margaret. I was named for my father's mother. Maggie stuck as a nickname but not for my father. He is the only one who calls me that." An unexpected feeling of tenderness for her father arose in Maggie.

"That is interesting. Well, you and I will meet once a week until the baby is born. I will make appointment for you with our doctors who come here Wednesday and Friday. I will accompany you on those visits. One of them will deliver your baby. This maybe a difficult time for you but I can assure you giving up the baby is the best thing you can do for it."

Maggie did not utter a sound, she felt like her jaws were locked in place. *Since when was my baby an 'it'.*

"I will ask you some questions about your health and background and what interest you may have."

Maggie watched and listened as Ann Marie's red lips moved with each question that was spoken with clarity. Maggie's answers were brief and to the point. No elaboration.

Ann Marie glanced at her watch. She lay down her pen and folded her hands. "We try hard to accommodate our girls and help them through this difficult time."

When the interview was over Maggie stood but did not turn to leave. Ann Marie looked up.

"Do we have to meet in your office? Can we meet outside?"

Ann Marie stiffened. "Well confidentiality is always a concern."

"Most of the girls I have met know whatever there is to know about me."

"I'll check and let you know but for the moment plan on meeting here."

"Okay. I like your earrings." Maggie said and left.

Ann Marie fingered an earring and frowned.

Maggie left and headed to the dining room for lunch. Ann Marie reopened Maggie's file and made several notations in the margin.

The dining room was cluttered with girls, some of whom Maggie had yet to meet. After picking up her food she found girls she knew to sit with and shared her story of meeting with Ann Marie.

"She said she's here to help me anyway she can. She seemed kind and told me I can see her anytime I want. She is coming with me to the doctor's visits too. She wears the biggest hoop earrings I have ever seen."

"I've seen those earrings; I wish I had a pair. She's one of the good ones. Acts like she really cares and she's always around. Sometime she even eats in here," said Caroline.

"I wish I got her," said Olivia.

After lunch the girls headed off to their various assignments and classes.

Maggie managed to keep busy with the library, classes, doctors' visits and socializing with the other girls which consisted of chats in the dining room, porch or lawn. She drank the delicious lemonade and shared her mother's brownies with Olivia and others. At meal time only milk was served.

Maggie was getting accustomed to institutional living. There was camaraderie amongst the girls. She looked forward to seeing them to hear about their classes, their doctors' visits and any news from home good or bad.

Her weekly meetings with Ann Marie were still held in the office with Ann Marie asking questions, writing in the note book and Maggie answering. On one such visit Maggie asked if Ann Marie had found out about meeting outside.

"Actually, I did and we can if that is what you like."

"Can we do it today?"

Ann Marie stood and gathered up her papers. Maggie led the way. After they were seated on the porch Ann Marie began.

"Tell me about your boyfriend?" Ann Marie asked.

"He was handsome and sweet but I am here and he's going off to college in September."

"I see. You will finish high school?"

"Yes. Do you have a boyfriend?"

Ann Marie inhaled and waited before answering. "Yes, I do. We are getting married in October."

"Who gets my baby?"

"We have lists of people who want babies but cannot have them."

"Are they kind and good?"

"We think so. They have to go through a rigorous check. Now then are you eating and sleeping."

"Is there someone waiting for my baby?"

"I don't know," said Ann Marie. "Maggie, I__"

"Yes."

"Never mind. I think we've had enough for the day."

To celebrate the Fourth of July a picnic was held with hot dogs, hamburgers, potato chips, soda and ice cream sundaes. Red and white checkered tablecloths were placed on picnic tables and the music from a record player gave it a festive air. Fireworks on the lawn completed the evening but the distraction was temporary. The girls were living without family surrounded by strangers who meant well. Each girl carried her own background different from each other yet their present situation bound them together in a unique relationship, one of caring and understanding.

Disappearances were common. Once a girl went into labor, she was whisked away, never to be seen again. It was as though the part of her life that was spent there never existed. She was sent home to resume her life as though nothing had happened. Jessica was absent from the Fourth of July picnic. It was common knowledge that her baby was due. No one spoke of her.

Maggie was assigned to the library which was open from two to four o'clock, Monday through Friday. It was called the library but it was a small room with four shelves containing the entire collection of books. A desk and a chair suitable for one person were next to the shelves. A metal case held index cards, one for each book. Maggie would write the date and the name of the girl on the card and file it until the book was returned. This solitary assignment suited Maggie. She read all the books and coaxed

Olivia to visit her. Maggie was full of suggestions for books that she thought Olivia might like.

The days and evenings moved swiftly but night time was Maggie's enemy. She lay awake thinking of her baby as it moved within her. A cool breeze came through the window and often she would look out at the stars and moon and talk to her baby saying they would get through this together and maybe one day they would find each other. She would never show her baby anything, where she lived, who the baby's grandparents were, who the father was. She had to leave something. Ann Marie said she would help her. She was overcome with despair at the thought of leaving her baby but she would come up with something if her baby wanted to find her. She clung to this thought.

Maggie's weekly appointment with dutiful Ann Marie who talked of exercise and good health for a pregnant woman was getting boring for Maggie. There was no discussion about birth or preparation of the grief that lie ahead. On one such meeting Maggie asked what the birth would be like. Ann Marie fell silent.

"I don't know. I have never had a child."

"Do you stay with me?"

"No. I take you to the hospital and come see you immediately after the baby is born. Usually they do just fine."

"How can they be 'just fine'?"

Ann Marie shrugged. "I guess__"

"They've given up their babies. How can they be 'just fine'?"

Ann Marie shifted in her seat.

"Will I be able to see my baby?"

"I'm not sure but I will make every effort to allow it."

"Please do. At least I can take that with me."

Joan arrived at Swan Point Home along with Ethan to visit Maggie. It was the middle of August. Ethan brought Maggie a note from George.

"George asked me to give this to you," he whispered so their mother wouldn't hear.

With a mixture of emotions she folded the note and tucked it in the pocket of her maternity top.

Later that evening Maggie lingered on the porch anxiously waiting for the rest of the girls to leave before she opened George's note. When at last she was alone, she unfolded the letter and read:

> August 25, 1957
> Dear Maggie,
> You were my first love. I miss you and think of you every day and night. When this is over maybe we can start our life again.
> Our friends ask about you and I told them you went away for a while. It's been good to see Ethan around makes me feel closer to you. I keep busy with work and sports but my heart isn't in it. I leave for college next month. We'll get through this and soon we'll be together again.
> Love, George.

He was her first love, too. Why did it turn out so bad, with her living with strangers and being forced to give up their baby? Looking out at the pond she watched as two swans glided by. The nest was near the shore. She crushed the letter, paused and then wrote back.

> August 31, 1957
> Dear George,
> I read your note and was glad to hear from you. You were my first love too.

Maybe we can find our baby someday. I have so much regret about this whole thing. Sometimes I wish I could start over and not be pregnant.

All this will be over soon but I will never forget it.

I will not be returning to Brant High, too many memories.

Good luck at college.

Maggie.

She folded the letter, placed it into an envelope and handed it to Ethan on his next visit.

"Give this to George when you see him."

Maggie was visiting with her mother and Ethan on the porch when Ann Marie walked up the steps. "May I join you?" she asked.

"Yes," said Joan.

Ann Marie pulled a chair over and sat down. "You don't have much longer to go, Maggie. How are you feeling?"

Surprised by this question, Maggie said. "Alright. I'm glad it will be over soon but leaving my baby will be hard."

Ann Marie held Maggie's hands in hers. "I promise you I will do everything I can to find a loving couple to adopt your baby." Ann Marie stood and entered the front door to Swan Point Home.

Chapter Four

❧

Maggie's attempts to get comfortable in bed were unsuccessful as she rolled from side to side. The baby reacted to all these movements by moving inside to its own position and comfort. A cramp coming from Maggie's back caused her to sit up. The baby's reaction was silence; movement within ceased at least for the moment when a definite, deliberate single movement crossed over her stomach. Was it a hand or a foot? Wham, another cramp, this one harder like the force of a gale wind. Maggie gasped. She felt something wet leaking from between her legs. When she stood up a puddle gathered on the floor and left a trail as she headed to the bathroom.

She stood on the cold bathroom floor holding on to the sink as the cramping enveloped her. Her bare feet were sticky from the fluid. She inspected her face in the mirror, the light in her eyes looked dim, her lips looked stiff and her honey blond hair had lost its gloss. She felt totally alone, all she had was herself. What little she had left of the feeling of joy was gone and in its place was sorrow. She couldn't go back; she couldn't erase what happened. She clung harder to the sink until the cramping stopped. She lessened her grip stood up straight and stared at her face in the mirror. She was seventeen. She felt bruised emotionally and knew she had left her carefree youth behind.

What will happen when they take my baby? Will I get to see it at all? Someone wants a baby and cannot have one. I am having a baby but cannot keep it.

She shook her head as more water trickled down her legs landing on the bathroom floor. *As long as the baby is right here, it's still with me but I have to give it away.*

During these months of waiting Maggie had wondered how she was going to feel when it was over. *I'm glad it's coming to an end but I wonder will it ever end, leaving the baby. What will happen when I go back to school? If anyone finds out will they not speak to me?*

Panic, a new emotion, enveloped Maggie. It was time to deliver her baby and afterward start her life over again. Holding her stomach she made it back to the bedroom and woke Olivia.

"What's the matter?"

"I think my water broke and I'm having real bad cramps."

Startled, Olivia got out of bed and crossed over to Maggie who was sitting on the edge of her bed. "What's it like?"

The girls held hands. "It hurts. But this is it; our babies will be taken from us soon," said Maggie.

"We're leaving our babies but at least you have a family to go back to. Me, I have nothing. No baby and no family."

"You can have a good future, Olivia. You've got to go on, for your own sake. Finish high school no matter what. Promise me that."

No one had ever said these kinds of things to Olivia, or believed in her, only Maggie.

Maggie dialed the number she had been given for emergencies. Soon there was a knock on the door. It was Ann Marie. "Come, Maggie, I'll help you get your things together. Are you alright?"

"I think so."

"The car is in the back. Just be careful on the stairs. I'll carry your things."

"Goodbye, Olivia," Maggie said and waited for her friend to respond.

Olivia sat there unable to move or speak and didn't cry until Maggie left, something she hadn't done in a long time.

Ann Marie pulled the car around to pick up Maggie who waited on the back steps. On the way to the hospital Maggie sat in the passenger seat and thought about her baby. Would her baby think she didn't want it? She wanted to let the truth be known. There must be a way. She must leave something. A letter, words from her heart that expressed how she felt. Someone would know where to put it...someone. She glanced at Ann Marie.

"I will be with you until the doctor examines you, then I will be back after the baby is born. Would you like me to call your mother?" Ann Marie asked. Maggie nodded. "If you want me to come at any time, just let the nurse know and I will be there. After the baby is born I will be with you every day," Ann Marie said as she laid her hand over Maggie's.

Upon arrival to the maternity floor, a nurse walked toward Maggie, "Can you walk?" she asked, looking at Maggie after examining the paper work.

"I guess so."

"Okay, follow me."

Holding on to her stomach Maggie followed the nurse into a room with two beds.

"Take off your clothes and put this on," the nurse said as she placed a hospital gown on the bed, turned and walked out. Between pains Maggie managed to remove her clothing, put on the bed gown and, shivering, got into bed. Alone, Maggie grieved; she yearned for a soothing word, a warm embrace, and a familiar voice. Thoughts of George crept into in her mind and she wondered where he was at this moment. Karen, her best friend, would they ever see each other again? She began to cry softly.

"We can do this baby, you and I. This is one thing they can't take away. Me giving birth to you," she whispered as she caressed her swollen belly.

After speaking with Ann Marie, Joan hung up the phone, woke Henry and left the house immediately promising to call him when it was over. Henry sat on the edge of the bed holding his head in his hands.

The next nurse Maggie saw introduced herself as Liz and gave her instructions about the delivery; what would happen and when it would happen.

"We'll give you some medicine to help ease the pain and I'm here until the afternoon but I'll tell you what if you're close to delivering I'll stay with you. You can have something to drink but no food. After you deliver we'll get you anything you want."

She hugged Maggie and said in her ear. "Don't worry, everything will be fine."

"It won't be fine. I'll have no baby."

"Yes, I know," said Liz sympathetically.

Maggie rolled over grabbed the side rails and yelled aloud. Every pain was bringing her to the end. But the end of what? Nine months. Was there a new beginning? What would that be? She envisioned holding her baby. She thought of names she would give it.

Liz came to her side and rubbing her back said. "Take deep breaths. Here, I'm putting a pillow between your legs; it may help you to relax."

"I can't relax. They're going to take my baby," Maggie sobbed. Her pains were coming closer and she knew that meant she was getting closer to seeing her baby; closer to losing her baby.

The doctor arrived, examined Maggie who was perspiring profusely, and ordered some medicine. "Actually, you're doing fine and your labor is progressing well. It's nearly over," he said.

But for Maggie it had just begun.

With Liz's suggestions and encouragement, her mother came to sit with Maggie. The medicine helped her doze between contractions until the sweeping pains came back.

When they subsided she looked at her mother through a haze.

"Mom, all this and no baby!" she cried.

The delivery was imminent. The nurse gave her more medicine. Maggie struggled to move onto the delivery table. She tried to focus on the people who seemed to be moving around her in slow motion. Their voices sounded distant. A haze surrounded her. Someone placed a mask over her face.

Maggie lifted her eyelids and blinked. Her bottom ached. She placed a hand over her flat stomach and realized the baby was gone. She turned her head toward an incubator. Inside was a squalling pink baby flailing its arms and kicking its legs. *Was it a boy or a girl?* The pale umbilical cord had been severed and tied with a clamp. The sight left an imprint on her heart. Her arms ached to hold her baby. This is all she had and perhaps she would never see it again. Their unmarked future was before them.

"It's over Maggie and you have a healthy and beautiful baby boy."

The date was September 2, 1957.

As Liz helped Maggie move from the delivery table to a stretcher her eyes never left the incubator. Liz covered her with a warm blanket and stopped. "Would you like to hold him?" she whispered.

Maggie pulled both arms from underneath the blanket holding her hands open. Liz lifted Maggie's baby out of the incubator and placed him in her arms; Maggie wept with joy and sadness. When Maggie held her baby and placed her lips on his forehead still damp from birth, snuggled him close and whispered in his ear, "I will remember you all the days of my life," his crying ceased. Maggie saw the resemblance to George just before Liz removed the baby from Maggie's arms and returned him to the incubator. *He's part of both of us.*

.

Three days later Maggie waited in her hospital room for Ann Marie who arrived every morning at ten o'clock. She felt like a shell carved out from life with nothing left inside. In Maggie's hand was an envelope that she stared at only to look up when Ann Marie walked in. Maggie eyes were fixed on the papers Ann Marie held in her hand knowing what they represented and with blurred vision she signed the necessary documents giving up her son.

Wiping her eyes with the back of her hand, she removed the four-leaf clover necklace from around her neck and placed it inside the envelope which contained a letter to her baby. On the outside of the envelope she wrote, Baby Boy Porter and handed it to Ann Marie.

"I want this to go with the adoption papers with instructions that if he comes looking for me this will be given to him."

"I will make sure of it," said Ann Marie.

Joan tried to discourage her but Maggie insisted and no one would refuse her this.

Maggie felt a connection to her baby unlike anything she'd experienced before. She had to put it out of her mind. She had to move on, but if she did, would she forget her baby? Her life had unraveled but the reweaving had begun, although she was unable to see it. She couldn't imagine anything breaking her heart as badly as this.

Chapter Five

The following day Maggie sat on the edge of her bed waiting for her mother and Ethan to come. Her baby was four days old. Her valiant attempt to hoist her spirits by concentrating on her future was failing her. She felt as if she had been swept away on a tidal wave of grief. The image of her baby was embedded in her heart. She clung to the one thought that could get her through the next minute, the next hour, and the next day; it was the last thread of hope that someday she would see him again

Ethan arrived, hugged Maggie and lifted her suitcase off the bed. There were no hand knit shawls, no toys to mark the occasion of her baby's birth, nothing but emptiness and unspoken feelings. Unshed tears lay beneath the surface waiting to moisten her cheeks.

"Come on Maggie, it's over," said her mother.

"It will never be over for me."

Ethan sat next to her on the bed. He placed his arm around her and waited. She stood up. Ethan took her by the hand and lead her out of the hospital.

"I'll bring the car around to the front door," said her mother.

The sun's brightness forced Maggie to shield her eyes as she went through the front door to the waiting car and climbed in followed by Ethan.

As her mother drove out of the hospital grounds, Maggie took a last look at the building she just left. Was her baby was still there or had he gone somewhere else? She suppressed an urge to yell at her mother to stop the car because she wanted to go back to see him just one more time. They drove home in silence. The car pulled into the driveway of the Porter home where from the outside everything looked the same but Maggie had changed. Her once carefree, cheerful demeanor was replaced by feelings of guilt, anger and sadness.

Did people ask where I was? How could someone go away for three months without anyone asking where they were?

Maggie approached the house. Her father opened the front door. "Mairead..."

Maggie looked at her father who appeared thinner, had lost a little more hair and there was no smile, he just nodded.

She walked past him and went to her bedroom. Her body ached, her bra was tight, her breasts were leaking and she was overwhelming tired. She glanced around her room which was the same as she left it. The only thing she welcomed was her soft bed and blue comforter, everything else was meaningless to her. She tossed George's school sweater on the floor, sat at her desk and tried to think. She had to return to school but which one? At some point she would have to leave the house and face people, what would they say, what would she say? She heard her mother's voice coming from downstairs.

"Maggie, supper is ready."

"I'll be right there," she answered.

Maggie entered the kitchen, familiarity overwhelmed her, but the nurturing days of sitting with her mother after school were over. She sat down at the table across from Ethan.

Joan served dinner; platters of food were passed around in awkward silence, three months of separation made conversation impossible.

Maggie pushed her food around on her plate. *Who is feeding my son?*

No one asked how she was or asked about the baby. It was if it never had happened.

"How is school going, Ethan?" she asked, her voice flat

"Ups and downs, you know."

"No, I don't."

"Have you thought about school, Maggie?" asked Joan

Maggie turned to her mother. "No, I've been busy." *Busy having a baby.*

"I spoke to the principal and he ...that is, we thought it would be better if you went to a private school."

Henry wiped his mouth with a napkin and waited.

"Fine. It doesn't matter. I'm ready to go back to school. The sooner the better."

"Good," Henry stated.

Maggie glared at her father. He stabbed a piece of chicken but it didn't make it to his mouth. He dropped his fork onto his plate and rubbed his chin.

"What's good about it, Dad?"

"School will be good, get your mind off things."

"What **things**?"

"I mean getting back with people your own age." He stood and headed to the sink with his plate.

"I've been with people my own age for three months."

Her mother froze, Ethan stopped eating, and her father turned his back to her.

"Do we have dessert, Joan?"

Maggie rose and left the table. Ethan followed her to her room and they both sat on the bed.

"Talk to me, Ethan."

"About what?"

"About anything. Basketball, movies, your classes, TV. Anything."

Ethan droned on about sports, school and his friends keeping a wary eye on Maggie, who stared straight ahead. He never mentioned George. She tried to pay attention but her thoughts pulled her elsewhere. The picture of her son was embedded in her mind and she could still feel the warmth of his little body and the softness of his forehead where she planted a kiss. From time to time she would look at Ethan and wonder if her son would resemble him: tall with light brown hair, blue eyes and a square chin.

Her first night home was the first of many nights in which Maggie tossed and turned, sometimes waking up because she thought she heard a baby cry. She would lay her hands across her belly once filled with life, now flat and quiet. Her arms ached to hold him. She dreamt he was adopted by a loving couple with another boy and the two would grow up together and be good friends. She was tormented by the thought that if she did see him again, she wouldn't know it was him. She clung to the thought that maybe he would look like George, that one day she would see a little boy who looked like him and she would instantly know it was her son.

Daytime rituals were school, homework and reading of novels. She avoided walks in the park, too many children.

"How's school going, Maggie?" asked her mother one day at breakfast.

"Fine."

"Are you meeting any new friends?"

"No, Mom. How am I going to tell them why I'm there and where I've been?"

"You could just say you were away and decided to go there when you came back."

"More lies, Mom? More made up stories? Where and when will it end?" Maggie stood and grabbed her coat and books and looked at her mother.

"Mom, I left part of me there, I wasn't just away. I had a baby who was part of you, too, in case you forgot."

"Maggie, please..."

"Please what, Mom? Forget? I never will."

She slammed the door shut and headed to school.

Maggie refused to go to church with her family. Occasionally she would watch TV with them if Ethan was there. Conversations with her parents were stilted to avoid arguments. Weekends she volunteered at the library in town. When children came in she would retreat to the bathroom and stand at the sink holding on, waiting for courage and swallowing hard to sooth her constricted throat. Were there more pregnant women around or was she imagining it? No matter where she went she was faced with reminders: pictures of babies splashed across the covers of magazines on display in stores, women pushing baby carriages, the sound of crying babies, some real, some imagined reverberated in her head. Finishing her last year of school was a passage in her life without acknowledgement, except for the diploma sent to her from school at her request.

Maggie mailed the last of her college applications and then began the wait. It wasn't long before she was accepted into the freshman class at Kent State University in Ohio.

She arrived on the campus in September, 1958. Cars were parked with trunks open to allow access to suitcases, lamps, typewriters and other items important to student life. The excitement of people her own age starting on their journey was palpable and thoughts of her baby and the past two years were lifted and in place was her future.

Maggie read the map and found her dormitory. With her family's help she unpacked her belongings and carried them to the second floor. There was chatter everywhere.

Upon entering the room Maggie drew back. Staring at her were twin beds with a night stand in between, two bureaus and a closet. Maggie thought of Olivia. *'I can't wait for this to be over.'* *Where was Olivia now?* A girl looked up from her suitcase, smiled and said. "Hi. I'm Leslie," bringing Maggie into the present.

Leslie was short and compact with long black hair that fell loose around her face. She unpacked her clothes removing each item and placing it in the bureau all the time speaking to Maggie in a soft even voice. "All the freshmen are invited to dinner in the cafeteria at five. Want to go together?"

"Yes, thanks. I'm Maggie."

Once the contents of the car had been delivered to Maggie's room, her mother started to unpack. Maggie placed her hand firmly on her mother's arm.

"Mom, it's okay. I'll unpack later. You should go. You have a long drive ahead of you."

Maggie turned to her father who was standing in the door-way threading the rim of his hat through his fingers. He looked at Maggie with wet eyes.

"Bye, Daddy."

Henry approached and kissed Maggie on the cheek. "Bye, Mairead."

The use of her given name which only her father used and the intimacy of the sound of it was like a secret shared between two people and feelings of comfort and belonging stirred in Maggie. The vision of her grandmother who was tiny, strong and sparse with her use of words and for whom she was named came to mind. Maggie returned her father's kiss with a kiss of her own on his cheek that was damp with tears.

Ethan stepped forward and wrapped his arms around Maggie. "Bye. I'll miss you but I promise I'll write."

"You'd better," Maggie said as she kissed his cheek. "And don't wipe it off."

Ethan chuckled as he left the room.

Maggie and Leslie took a walk around campus. New construction of dormitories and academic buildings were everywhere. They passed the new Student Union which housed pool tables, a bookstore, cafeterias, lounges and a faculty dining room. They went in and joined other freshmen who were seated at large round tables. Posted on the wall in back of the buffet was a sign welcoming freshmen.

"Gosh, Maggie can you imagine? Look at this place, it's huge. Think of all the people we'll meet and all the exciting things we'll learn. I can't wait. We have everything to look forward to."

"Yes, we do," said Maggie

Yes, Maggie had everything to look forward to; a new beginning, a fresh start. How would she adjust to this life? She would, she had to. Her past still weighed her down but Leslie's enthusiastic attitude was uplifting.

They returned to the dorm and put away the last few things, made their beds and lay on top of them. Freshmen orientation would take place the next day.

"So, what courses are you going to take?" asked Leslie.

"Well I'm hoping for a degree in Library and Information Science."

"A librarian. Good. When I have kids I can tell them my college roommate was a librarian."

Maggie took a deep breath turned on her side and waited for sleep. Anxiety about embarking on a new experience clung to Maggie like cat hair on a black sweater and did not disappear with the arrival of dawn.

The following morning Maggie attended freshmen orientation which lasted until three o'clock. Students spoke of clothes they would wear, classes they would take, what games they would attend, their boyfriends back home and the cute boys they had seen already. They compared high school class rings. *I'll have to avoid these conversations as much as possible. I have a story but it is not about clothes, boyfriends and class rings.*

The days turned into weeks in which Maggie thrived in the college environment. In class, her hand went up first and her enthusiastic attitude was contagious to her classmates. Her frequent visits to the library soon had the staff calling her by her first name. Her old self was emerging. On occasion she would wonder how George was doing. What college did he go to? Did he ever think of her? She rubbed her temples erasing these thoughts. Saturday morning she ran three miles, returned to the dorm, showered, studied and wrote to Ethan. No amount of coaxing by Leslie could entice anything social for Maggie. Her lack of interest made her appear cool and reserved by her classmates. The invitations dwindled.

The night before they were to leave for Thanksgiving break, Leslie awoke to the sound of Maggie's voice. "No give him back. I want him back. He's mine," she shouted, tossing and turning.

"Maggie, Maggie." Leslie gently shook her friend, "Hey, hey."

Maggie opened her eyes; the look on her face was frantic. Her hand was on her throat and she was panting.

"What was that all about? Some dream you were having," said Leslie.

"It was a dream but it really happened." Maggie rose, situated herself in bed and hugged her pillow. Leslie waited sitting cross legged on her bed wondering whatever could have caused these nightmares that she had been witnessing since September.

Maggie starting talking, cautiously at first, then words tumbled out of her mouth like a waterfall, there was no stopping them. "They sent me away. I had to live with people I didn't know for three months and give up my baby." Tossing the pillow aside she exclaimed. "When I came home there was no talk of where I had been or what took place."

Maggie talked for two hours. When she finished she let out a long sigh. The guilt had been evicted, the oppressive weight in her chest lifted.

"That is why I have nightmares."

"Oh, my God. That's incredible. It's gotta be the worst thing. I've heard about girls who had babies and weren't married that were sent away. I never knew one." She looked at Maggie. "You must be so strong."

"Not always. Secrets make you weak and scared. Coming here has been good though. It's the first thing that has excited me, sort of like my life before the baby. I can't go out with anyone. What if he finds out and tells everyone? Besides I don't want to go out. My classes are enough right now."

"Do you still think about the Father of the baby?"

"Sometimes. I wrote him an answer to his letter but I never heard back from him so I guess he found other things to do. He must be a sophomore at college now."

"He probably got caught up in wild fraternity parties like most college guys. Let it go, Maggie. Get you own social life. Eventually you will date. Right? I mean everyone dates!"

"Maybe, but not just yet...maybe in the future," Maggie said as she slipped under the covers. Her last thought before falling asleep was of George.

After that night there were no secrets between the roommates. Maggie found peace with Leslie. She could share her thoughts knowing it would stay between them.

Maggie shunned boys who showed the least bit of interest until they no longer inquired. She wondered if she would ever date again. How would she respond? What kind of a boy would appeal to her and what would they do if they knew her secret? It was all too much to think about.

Maggie stayed at school for the Thanksgiving holiday. The cafeteria was decorated with live pumpkins and the staff wore aprons with pictures of turkeys on the front. Dinner was celebrated with other freshman including Leslie and the next night they all headed into town to see *Peyton Place*.

Christmas was fast approaching. In town, trees were adorned with white lights; tiny silver ornaments clung to their branches. And then there were the children; excited, wide eyed, with open mouths whose mothers pulled them away from all the distraction. Her son would be walking and she imagined his excitement with Christmas and Santa Claus.

Henry and Ethan drove to Ohio to bring Maggie home for Christmas. Maggie's anger and hurt and Henry's disappointment and hurt had begun to thaw which allowed them to converse without judgment or rancor.

The Porter house was full for Christmas dinner with family and friends. Maggie was starting to feel whole again.

The next day she called Karen whom she had not seen since she left to have the baby.

"Maggie, is it really you? It's so good to hear from you. It's been over a year."

"It's good to hear your voice, Karen. I'm sorry it took so long."

"That's okay. I figured you would call when you were ready. Are you in college?"

"Yes, Kent State, I needed to get away, it's been good for me and my roommate is great. How about you?"

"I ended up going to Boston University. I love Boston. It's full of young people__"

"Karen, I had a boy a year ago last September."

"Oh Maggie. How was it? I mean having the baby and giving it up? I thought of you many times."

"It will be with me forever, Karen."

"I don't know what to say. It must have been so hard."

"How was graduation?"

"Fun, I mean it was fine, you know."

"No I don't know. I didn't go to mine."

"Oh."

After they had exhausted their conversation they promised to write and hung up the phone but neither of them spoke of getting together.

Maggie's father drove her to the bus station for her trip back to Kent State, and waited until she boarded.

"Did you enjoy yourself at home?" he asked.

"I did Daddy. It was good to be here."

"Mairead, I'm sorry..."

"Daddy. It's okay."

"I did what I thought was best."

"I know, I know."

Henry wrapped his arms around Maggie, she placed her cheek on his chest and he kissed the top of her head.

"Here's my bus, Daddy. I'll write."

Maggie completed freshman year and decided to stay in town for the summer because she was not ready to spend the summer in the environment of memories and she wanted to get the feel of being on her own, which meant getting a job. The local sandwich shop was hiring and she headed there to apply.

After reading Maggie's application, the man raised his thick eyebrows and said, "We like students from Kent, can you start Monday?"

"I can."

"Lookin' for a place to rent for the summer?"

"Yes. Do you know a place?"

"Sure do. My wife's brother has some rooms he rents to kids like you. The kitchen is shared but you have your own room. Here's his number. It's within walking distance from my shop so no excuses for being late."

Maggie greeted customers at the shop with a smile and once she got to know them she called them by name. At last she was enjoying something. When she wasn't there they asked where she was. Her cheerful demeanor was returning.

Thoughts of her baby receded somewhat when she returned for sophomore year, but regrettably something always triggered reminders of him: a book store with a children's section reminding her that she never would buy a book for him, passing a children's store and wondering if he had his first pair of shoes yet. Was he walking and playing with trucks? She would entertain these thoughts but it was getting easier to switch channels.

Focusing on her studies became her prime interest, until Leslie told her about auditions being held for the spring performance of Macbeth.

"Leslie, I don't have time. Besides what do I know about acting?"

"This isn't New York, it's college theater. You need a little fun in your life. Let loose. All you do is study. Here we are in the middle of sophomore year and your classes are going fine."

At Leslie's insistence Maggie auditioned and was surprised when she was chosen to play the part of Lady Macbeth. She received rave reviews in the college newspaper about her acting debut. *"A solid moving performance by an amateur and one that we look forward to seeing again."* Playing the part suited her. Guilt was part of who she was.

In June, Maggie went home for Ethan's graduation from high school. Her mother fussed, her father made her pancakes on Saturday morning with fresh maple syrup, and Ethan spent all his free time with her. Words that were said and actions taken, all in the house, were reminders of what took place but deliberately ignored. The family chose to bury the past. At Ethan's graduation no one remembered her, a fact for which she was grateful.

She returned to Kent State and spent the rest of the summer living in the apartment house with other students, and working at the sandwich shop. If her friends were going to the movies or out for pizza she would join them, but dates were out, she wasn't ready. Upon her return to college, Leslie told Maggie point blank that she needed to come out of her self-imposed social exile and start dating.

"Who am I supposed to date, Eric who has roving hands? I've seen him in action. Or Mark who always looks at the girls with big chests? No thanks."

"Look, it's the start of junior year and our friends are going to the tavern tonight. You go out with the people at the sandwich shop so why not the Tavern?"

"Oh, Leslie."

"Don't 'oh Leslie' me. You're coming and if you don't they'll all end up here in our apartment. You don't want that with the first year of living off campus, do you?"

"Well, I guess I'll go."

That evening they walked to the tavern and when they entered, Sal, the owner, called out.

"Hey Leslie. This must be Maggie. You finally got her to come here."

"Yeah, so don't mess it up."

Maggie grinned as she slid into a booth not realizing someone was already there sitting across from her. She looked up to see a man sipping a beer.

"Oh, sorry. Are you saving this for someone?" she asked.

"Yes, you. Be my guest." His curly brown hair partly covered his ears. His bushy eyebrows did not diminish his brown eyes which stared at her making her quake under their intense gaze.

"And who might you be?" Leslie asked sliding in next to Maggie.

"Joe Carlson." He looked directly at Maggie and asked in a deep resonant voice,

"And who might you be?"

Leslie came to rescue. "She's Maggie and I'm Leslie. Roommates since freshman year."

"Joe Carlson. I'm a second year grad student."

"Do you read the college newspaper?" Leslie asked. Maggie knew what Leslie was doing.

"As a matter of fact I do."

"You're looking at Lady Macbeth---end of sophomore year. I'll leave you two to get acquainted."

Maggie felt panicky. *Don't leave Leslie I can't do this. I'll get you for this.* She turned toward her friend, grabbed her wrist and pinched it. Leslie broke loose. "Bye, bye."

"So, Lady Macbeth, did you enjoy the part?" Joe asked.

"Yes, I did. She had such remorse for her misdeeds and never forgave herself but it wasn't all her doing."

"But she did go along with it."

"Sometimes people have no choice. Guilt is not an easy thing to live with but suicide. You can never redeem yourself. The part forced me to look at guilt and the way it can encompass your life if you're not careful."

"Well you certainly played it well."

If he only knew.

The dreaded lapse in conversation occurred.

She felt him staring at her but kept her eyes focused on the waitress who was waiting on the table next to them.

"Would you like to order something? I see you are staring at the waitress. Are you hungry?" he asked, searching her face.

"No," Maggie said.

"Would you like something to drink?"

"No, thanks. Well, maybe a beer. Yes, yes, a beer would be fine."

"Waitress!" he called waving his hand. "A beer for Lady Macbeth."

When he turned to do this Maggie took a good look at his profile and liked what she saw, a long nose and hair resting on the neck of his sweater. He was handsome and husky.

"Now then, Lady Macbeth, tell me about you. What do you like to do?"

"Please call me Maggie." She managed a smile and started to relax.

"Okay."

The waitress arrived with the beer and set it down.

"What are you studying in graduate school?" she asked, diverting the attention away from her.

"Journalism. I came here to attend the Annual Short Course in Photojournalism and decided to go to grad school. Hope to finish next year. Eventually I would like to do television reporting. Actually I work for the college newspaper and I wrote the column about your appearance in Lady Macbeth after I saw your performance. You were impressive."

She had just taken a sip of beer and managed to swallow it without a disaster occurring. She wiped her lips and started to laugh. He held up his glass to hers. "Here's to us." Maggie raised hers.

After that night, Maggie and Joe spent all their free time together. They talked, went to movies, and Friday nights were spent eating spaghetti in Maggie's apartment. Maggie's social reserve was slipping away but a close personal relationship was out of her reach.

Maggie spent Christmas at home with her family. She purchased sweat shirts with the name Kent State printed on them, navy for her father and tan for Ethan who proceeded to pull them over their heads and strut around the living room as Maggie and her mother agreed that the fit was perfect. For her mother she purchased stationery with the Kent State logo. The old grievances were never discussed. They remained dormant. It seemed better that way at least for now.

The evening before the start of second semester, Maggie and Leslie sat at the kitchen table in their apartment sharing a pizza.

"Okay, out with it," stated Leslie.

"Out with what?" said Maggie obviously irritated.

"You've been seeing Joe since the beginning of junior year and now all of a sudden I've got a cranky roommate."

"Can't I be cranky once in a while? You're not exactly Miss Perfect all the time either," she shot back at Leslie.

"Look, I know you. You're holding something back and it's making you nuts and your moods are making me nuts. What is it?"

"It's nothing. I'm tired. Now please just leave me alone."

"You're my best friend and I know something is bothering you. If you want to talk I'm here. That's all."

Maggie relaxed. "I'm sorry."

"It has to do with Joe. Am I right?"

Maggie nodded. "He's a great guy and he's all I think about, but..."

"I think I know the rest. You've haven't told him about the baby."

Maggie nodded. "I'm afraid he'll end our relationship. I knew I would have to face this sooner or later."

"Not if I know Joe. If he loves you it won't matter. You've got to tell him and do it soon. At least then you can go from there but until you tell him you'll be miserable. Relationships are built on trust and honesty."

The next weekend, after seeing *West Side Story*, Maggie suggested they take a walk through the park; Joe put his arm around Maggie and pulled her close. "Great movie," he said.

"Yes it was. Joe, I've got to talk to you."

"I figured something was up. You've been distracted lately."

"I have?"

"Yes. Let's sit over here on this bench and you can tell me what's bothering you."

She looked directly at him, "Joe something happened to me a long time ago which I think I should tell you about."

"And that is?"

Maggie told Joe her story. Her fear associated with her pregnancy, her anger at her father, and her sorrow giving up her baby. The loneliness living away from her family and the difficulty coming back, no social life, no friends, just Ethan. Each layer Maggie unfolded was accompanied by relief that freed up the demons of loss and guilt. Joe's expression never changed. He waited until he was sure she was finished.

"Maggie, you never mentioned the father. Do you still think about him?"

"I haven't seen him since I went away. He knew about the baby and went to college. Our parents forbade us from seeing each other and we haven't had any contact since then. I don't know where he is now." The hurt started to rise again like bile in her throat. She swallowed hard. "Meeting and being with you has been the best thing that happened to me since then."

"That's all I need to hear. I love you, Maggie." Joe placed his hands on Maggie's cheeks and kissed her before she could say another word.

"I love you, too, Joe. I was so afraid you would break it off."

"Marry me."

Marriage, commitment. I promised myself I would not let anything get in the way of college. I have another year to go. And yet...I love this man and he loves me.

"Yes, I will. But, Joe I must finish college first. You understand?"

"I can wait."

Chapter Six

❧

Maggie sat back, laid her pen down and looked out the window. The sun was high on this June day and roses dazzled the campus with their hue and size. Her last exam was over and she was done with college. Her son would be starting kindergarten this fall.

Walking to the front of the classroom she handed her paper to the professor and before she reached the door he called to her.

"Maggie, you forgot the last page of questions." He handed the paper back to her and said. "You're one of the best students I've had in a while. I've watched you from freshman year evolve into a fine young woman, but your mind always seems to be elsewhere. I've had you in prior classes and this has not changed, must be something heavy."

"Thank you, Professor Smith. It's nothing," she answered and took the papers to her seat to finish.

She was breathing rapidly, beads of sweat rounding her hairline. *Will this constant worry--where he is and how he is ever end? I should have fought my parents more. I wonder if he knows about me and if he does, what did his adoptive parents tell him about me?*

She hurried through the last page of questions and fled outdoors.

The following Saturday Maggie joined her classmates as they took their turn parading across the stage to receive their diplomas amidst cheers and hoots, and imagining she could hear Ethan and Joe yelling her name.

That evening, Maggie and Leslie celebrated their graduation at their apartment with family and a few friends. Joe pulled Maggie aside and whispered in her ear.

"Now will you marry me?"

"Yes, I will." she laughed.

"How about next weekend? I don't want you to change your mind."

"But Joe do we have enough time to get everything done?"

"I've made most of the arrangements just waiting for the green light from you. Everyone is here. Let's do it. Let's tell them. Let's be happy, Maggie."

Maggie turned to look at all the people in her life who meant so much to her. Joe was right. This was the perfect time to make their announcement.

"Attention everyone." Heads turned, waiting. "Joe has asked me to marry him and I said yes."

A roar came from the crowd. Ethan raised both arms, Leslie clapped her hands together, Joan grinned from ear to ear, and even Henry smiled.

Maggie pulled Ethan to a corner of the room and slipped her arm through his.

"I never thought I would get over George but I did. I hope you find someone as wonderful as I did."

"Joe's a lucky guy. By the way, Maggie. Try to let up on Dad; it was a long time ago. He loves you."

"I know he does."

Joe gladdened her heart and helped her climb her mountain of fears and look at them one by one. She loved him and the love he returned to her was like a river bathing her in comfort and peace and she welcomed it.

Maggie spent the following week shopping for a dress, an outfit for her mother and Leslie, shoes and flowers and gave careful consideration to the caterer, music and a church which Joe had arranged. She and Joe chose plain gold wedding bands. Everything was in place and the wedding party stood outside of church admiring each other's appearance while waiting to go in.

Standing at the back of church holding her father's arm she mused that her son would have made a handsome ring bearer. Burying that thought, she looked down the aisle away from her father toward Joe. Happiness filled in the spaces of regret.

Maggie and Joe clung to each other while thanking everyone for coming and promising to keep in touch. Her mother had eaten little and seemed listless through all the festivities. Noticing this Maggie nudged Ethan.

"Mom doesn't look so good. She's looks tired."

"Probably the trip and being up later than usual. Good thing you and Joe are moving back home. It will be a comfort for them."

What was a comfort for me?

Joe and Maggie rented a second floor apartment ten miles from Henry and Joan. They furnished it with purchases from the local second hand store. Their one extravagance was the new furniture for the bedroom, not wanting to sleep in someone else's bed. Maggie would race to the window when she heard Joe's car pull into the driveway. He would announce himself when he opened the door, "Hello, I'm home."

She would answer, "Hello, I'm here." They would kiss and embrace. Time felt endless to the young couple. They always seemed to have plenty of it for walks in the park, movies, books, and discussing their future.

One night Joe asked Maggie if she ever thought about the father of the baby.

"No. What we thought was love was adolescent passion. We were blind to the consequences. But we still had a child together."

"Maggie it's been five years. You have to forget and get on with your life. We're together now and we'll have our own family. You've got to start forgetting him."

"That won't happen, Joe. He was part of me. Maybe someday I'll get to see him. If I knew he was okay things would be different. Then, maybe, I could forget. But it's the not knowing that bothers me and probably always will. Before I met you I thought I would never be happy again. Also I was afraid to give myself over to another person, but you changed that for me. And, yes we will have our own family."

"Is that an invitation?" he asked with a wicked grin.

"It certainly is." And she threw herself into his arms.

The following week at the library, Maggie was restocking books waiting for her preschoolers to arrive for story time when she looked up to see her mother walk in.

"Mom, what a surprise." Maggie hugged her and felt her thin body beneath her jacket.

"Are you okay? Come sit here."

"I'm fine. I just need to talk to you."

Maggie noticed the absence of color in her mother's face and a slight tremor in her hands, more pronounced now than at the wedding.

"I wonder if we could go somewhere to talk."

"Of course. I'll ask Laura to do my story hour. We can go to the coffee shop around the corner. Is everything okay? You look a little tired, Mom."

"Actually I am a little tired."

"Stay here. I'll get my coat and be right back."

Maggie ordered coffee for herself and tea for her mother.

"Now, tell me what's bothering you."

Joan looked at her daughter and laid her delicate fingers on Maggie's arm.

"I've been to see Dr. Brown and the news wasn't good."

The waitress arrived with coffee and tea, placed the cups, milk and sugar on the table and left.

"What news? Mom, what are saying?"

"I have cancer."

Maggie's hands went to her face.

"No, no. We have to see another doctor. There must be some mistake..."

"No, Maggie. There's no mistake. I've had all the tests."

Maggie was speechless, she glanced around the coffee shop hoping someone would tell her this was not so, that her mother did not have cancer and they would sit in the kitchen again eating brownies but no one came forward. Her eyes rested on her mother's face. There was a peacefulness there that Maggie didn't notice because she only saw how tired and pale her mother looked.

"I wanted to tell you myself, just the two of us. I thought it would be better that way. Your father is heartbroken and he will need you."

"Don't worry, I'll look after him and help you. What do you need, Mom?" Maggie said as she choked back tears."

"I need you to be strong for me and I will be strong for you. When Ethan comes home from college this weekend I will tell him."

They drank their drinks and Maggie took the rest of the day off to be with her mother.

After saying goodbye to Maggie, Joan arrived home walked to the desk in her living room and rummaged through papers, her hands trembling she removed an envelope yellow with age and unable to destroy it placed it back into the desk.

For the next few months the family lived with uncertainty. How long would Joan live? What would they be able to do for her? Would she be in pain? Maggie rose to the occasion. With the help of Dr. Brown she contacted a hospice program and thus learned how to care for someone she loved who would eventually die which reminded her of carrying a baby and loving it only to have to give it away.

Maggie scheduled nursing visits and visited her mother after work every day. Often she would bring custard tarts that Joan was fond of. If Joan was too tired to read Maggie would read to her. She brushed her mother's hair and applied night cream to her face. Maggie told Joan about her work and her life with Joe. She encouraged her mother to eat. Ethan came home from college every other weekend and called every Wednesday to keep in touch.

Henry was devastated that he was losing his wife. At Maggie's insistence he continued to work and kept his normal routine. His reliance on Maggie increased daily by small increments until he was fully dependent on her. Maggie continued to include him in the care of Joan and insisted he participate.

"Dad, we have to take care of Mom. You can't change what is."

"I'm lost, Maggie. I can't do this," her father said. They were seated at the kitchen table. Maggie leaned forward and in a clear voice said. "Dad, Mom needs us. I'm right here. We'll do it together. Now scramble Mom an egg and I'll get her tea ready. When we are in front of her we keep the conversation upbeat. If she changes the subject we go with it."

Henry pushed back his chair and went in search of the frying pan.

One afternoon when sitting with her mother, Joan feebly reached for Maggie's hand and missed. Maggie caught it, her heart breaking to feel her mother's hand so cold and frail.

"Maggie," she whispered, "I'm sorry for what happened you know with the baby. Forgive me. You and Joe are so happy. I know you will have another baby and it will be the right time. You were so young...so young. We were wrong to leave him. I think of him every day. Can you ever forgive me?" Joan's voice faded as she covered her eyes with her arm. "He was so beautiful."

Maggie stood and covered her face with her hands. For the first time since the baby was born six years ago her mother spoke of him acknowledging her complicity. With this admission Maggie laid down her arms; a truce had begun.

Maggie spoke in a monotone, soft but clear. "He was ours and yes, we should not have let him go. It will be with me forever. You did what you had to do, Mom."

"We lost a member of our family," her mother said weakly. "I should have insisted we keep the baby but it was the time, the time. I hope he is alright. I never stopped worrying about him."

"Maybe someday he'll find me and I can make it up to him." It was a lost opportunity for reconciliation. Joan didn't hear for she had taken her last breath.

Maggie sat motionless and watched her mother's lifeless body. All those years of silence; there was so much unsaid. The past lay buried.

The following days brought the distraction of funeral arrangements and details to be attended to but Maggie's last conversation with her mother ruminated in her mind. *She did worry about her grandson and wonder where he was. If I had known we could have talked about it.* Ethan's arrival was a great source of comfort to Maggie and seemed to alleviate the nausea and tiredness which overwhelmed her.

After the funeral Maggie stayed in the house with her father for a few days, helping him go through her mother's things and getting the house back in order.

One evening sitting in the living room Maggie was going through the mail and asked her father if he was caught up with his bills.

He looked at her, frowning. "I don't know. Check the desk."

Maggie went to the desk where her parents kept their papers. The top came down revealing several cubbyholes containing stamps, paper clips, envelopes and a stack of unopened mail. There were two drawers below the desk top. Maggie slid open the first. This contained bank statements and the deed to their house. The second drawer contained their will, and a picture of her and Ethan taken the first day of school. In the picture Ethan was the age her son would be now. Maggie read some cards they had sent to their parents and smiled remembering those days and was about to close the drawer when she saw an envelope at the back. Pulling it out she saw it was addressed to her. She opened it and read the following:

> Dear Maggie,
> I still think of you every day. I hope you are alright. I started college in September so I haven't seen Ethan who kept me up to date on you. Getting over you isn't easy for me and I would like to see you sometime. My address at college is in the left hand corner. Please write to me and let me know if it's okay to call you when I come home. If I don't hear from you I'll know that I shouldn't call.
> George.

The postmark was November, 1957. Maggie started trembling and her face turned scarlet, her eyes became slits and her heart pounded. *It validates the love he felt but hope was lost when I didn't respond.*

She walked into the living room where Henry was sitting. He looked up.

"Well, how were the bills?" he asked.

"Fine. What's this?" She waved the letter at her father.

"Let me see it."

She handed it to him.

He glanced over the letter and placed his hand over his forehead and looked up at Maggie. "I can explain..."

"Explain what? You shut him out of my life. You forced me to give up my baby and now this. He must have felt terrible. The least I would have done was to write to him. You had no right to keep this from me."

Henry stood. "I did what I thought was best. I did not want him in your life. Can you understand that? What I did, I did for you."

"You did it for me? You did it for yourself! You wanted everything the way you thought it should be. Not once did you think of me. All these years of thinking you were doing what's best for me, did you ever think about what I thought was best for me? I grieve every day for a baby I'll probably never know. He is part of me and if I ever find him or he finds me I'll do what is best for me and him."

Henry looked at her. "You think he might find you?"

"Anything's possible. And if he does I'll welcome him with open arms. I understand what you and Mom must have gone through when I got pregnant but__"

Henry winced and held up his hand. "Don't__"

"Don't what, Dad? Talk about a situation that happened that affected all of us probably for the rest of our lives? Not to mention how it affected my son. Don't you see? Not talking about it and hiding it only makes it smolder like warm ashes and eventually a fire starts because the heat is overwhelming, just like it did now when I found the letter. At least now, maybe we can talk about it. Mom talked about my son just before she died."

"She did!"

"Yes and said she was sorry. I don't need you to say that Dad, but when I talk about it just listen and try to understand how I felt about giving up my son."

Maggie knelt in front of her Father.

"Dad, I've replaced anger and resentment with understanding and acceptance. Mom is gone and we need each other. The past is past but I'll never forget him and I realize why you and Mom did what you did."

Maggie continued getting the place in order, using a monotone voice to enlist her father's help who moved sluggishly around mourning his wife's passing.

"Dad, this is your house. I need to go back to mine. Joe and I are close by. Visit us whenever you want or we can visit you here. You also have Ethan to think of."

"I know, I know."

"Sometime life is hard, Dad." She stared at her father.

Chapter Seven

❧

Maggie's mother's death and the conversation with her father sucked the last sap of energy from her body. She crawled out of bed in the morning, languished around the house waiting for the dark robe of night to come to ease her sorrow. She would lie in bed with her book open, infrequently turning the pages without anticipation as to what was on the next page.

It will never be over until I know where he is. Maybe I will never know. Secrets keep us from being who we are.

Maggie eased out of bed and headed for the bathroom and peered into the mirror. She hadn't showered in days and her hair was a tangled mess. She tore off her pajamas and turned the shower on full force. The water streamed over her body. She lathered her hair. The washing and rinsing floated away the sawdust in her head. She stepped out of the shower, towel dried and dressed.

I must get something to eat or drink. I'm so tired.

Passing Joe's bureau she noticed a pocket calendar open to April, turning the pages back to March then February she realized she had not had a period since January, there could only be one cause, a pregnancy, hers and Joe's.

"Joe, Joe." She called out as she flew down the stairs.

"What is it?" he asked.

"I think I'm pregnant!"

"What?"

"Pregnant, Joe, pregnant."

Joe lifted Maggie up in his arms and set her down gingerly.

"This is great news!" Joe said as he folded Maggie's body into his and kissed her gently on the lips.

Great news, how different the reaction. Last time it was fear and anxiety. This one I'll get to hold, feed and walk in the park. No one will take this baby from me.

Joe released her.

"We better call a doctor. How about some scrambled eggs, a slice of toast? Oh my God, I'm going to be a father."

Maggie thought back to the experience of her first pregnancy, so void of any joy. In the beginning she ran a race against time trying to conceal it, knowing the revelation would release torrents of emotions none of which would be good. This pregnancy grew and she relished it, wearing maternity clothes before she needed them, browsing through baby stores discussing cribs and clothes and books with the store clerk with whom she became friendly. Maggie and Joe would eventually buy enough stuff for two babies.

"Joe, sometimes I get scared something is going to happen. I know it sounds ridiculous but it's real."

"Maggie, settle down. It's okay, nothing's going to happen. I'll be with you."

"It's all coming back. The anguish I felt because the baby would be taken away. I can feel it now. Seven years ago and I can still call it up".

"Look, why don't I leave work early today and we can organize the room. I just hope the kid can fit in there after all the stuff we've bought."

Joe painted the room, the crib was placed near the window and tiny garments, which Maggie folded and refolded, found their way into the bureau. The rocking chair was a catharsis for Maggie, where she sat and rocked welcoming the relief of sadness associated with a longing for her son which was replaced by thoughts of this new baby.

It was two o'clock in the morning and Maggie slipped out of bed, her large belly made the movement awkward and went downstairs to make some tea. She gazed out of the window to see a full moon and a sky laden with stars. The ground had begun to soften after the winters freeze and the stream had started a trickle. She turned off the gas and was interrupted by a strong cramp that started in her back, crawled around her sides and landed in her stomach.

"Joe, Joe!" she yelled. Joe came down the stairs two at a time.

"What? Are you okay?"

"Yes, I'm in labor."

Joe called the doctor, wrapped a coat around Maggie's shoulders and ran to warm up the car. He helped her in and they drove off.

"Don't leave me, Joe."

"Of course not. A linebacker couldn't keep me away."

"Breathe with the pain, Maggie," the nurse said.

"That's it, Maggie, just breathe," Joe repeated.

Desperately needing reassurance Maggie yelled aloud, "They won't take the baby away will they?"

"Not a chance." Joe wiped her forehead with a damp cloth.

Maggie dozed and dreamt of strangers gathering around her bed, calling to her but all she heard was baby, baby.

She woke and screamed at the nurse. "Don't take my baby!"

"I certainly won't. I have two at home and that's enough."

"Joe, I'm trying not to be scared."

"Yes, I know."

"Okay, Maggie you're ready. A couple of pushes and you're done."

A baby girl, wrapped in a blanket, was placed in Maggie's arms. Tears formed in the corner of Maggie's eyes. The baby's soft cry fell on Maggie's ears. Maggie placed her lips on the baby's soft, fragile forehead still damp from birth. She moved her fingertip across the baby's mouth and chin. The feel of the small baby in her arms provided unimaginable peace and unconditional love. Tiny fingers wrapped around Maggie's forefinger and her heart.

They named her Frances. Maggie sat up nights with the baby comforting her when she cried. During the day she watched Frances's every move. She whispered in the baby's ear, telling her stories. Frances responded by lifting her head and letting it rest on Maggie's shoulder. Frances put her tiny fist in her mouth trying to suck on it until Maggie switched her to nurse. Every sound made by the baby fueled Maggie's maternal instinct causing her to respond by holding her baby close to her heart.

Two years later Maggie and Joe presented Frances with a sister. They named her Emma.

Caring for her two daughters and Joe, Maggie was never happier. They made castles and animals with Play Dough. Frances made necklaces from Pop Beads, even for Joe which he proudly wore. Maggie read *A Snowy Day* by Ezra Jack Keats over and over again. Every day they took walks in the park and watched squirrels chew acorns. Maggie poured love and attention onto Frances and Emma hoping somewhere her son was receiving the same; that he was happy, that he was loved and that he was safe.

PART TWO

Chapter Eight

❦

Julia O'Brien sat up in bed, pulled her long red hair to one side and slid her feet into her shoes. Her skin was fair with the exception of freckles which crossed the bridge of her nose to her high cheek bones. Two open suitcases were lined up under her bedroom window and she looked at them with excitement; today she was leaving Ireland for America to join her brother, Tom. For one last time she checked the suitcases, zippered them closed and glanced out of the window to see her brothers helping their father bring in the cows and watched the dogs corral the sheep. They worked from sun up to sun down as they had since leaving school.

Am I doing the right thing? Leaving everyone I love? But Tom is there and I have a job waiting for me so how bad can it be? I've never lived anywhere else but here. I'm so excited I can hardly think.

Julia glanced at her two sleeping sisters and planted a kiss on each cheek. She stood, left the bedroom and flew downstairs almost losing her balance.

The turf fire was blazing in the large stone fireplace. Alongside the wall, adjacent to the fireplace, was a wooden bench. A pot of oatmeal was dangling over the fire at the end of a crane. Julia's mother was pouring tea and slicing Irish bread. A slab of butter glistened on a plate. Mary O'Brien had wrapped a loaf of the bread for Julia to take with her on the trip.

"Good morning, darlin', everything's ready. Now sit here and enjoy your breakfast," invited her mother. "Mr. Hennessey will be here in an hour to drive you to Shannon."

Julia sat at the long wooden table where the family shared their meals. Clean plates and cups were stacked on the counter. Underneath were two shelves one for knives, forks and spoons and one for pots. Over the large kitchen sink a window provided extraordinary views of rolling hills, patchwork of green hues and cows grazing in the distance.

Julia got up from the table and looked out of the window sipping her tea gazing at the vistas she had seen all of her life. For generations her family had farmed this land but where was her place here? There was only so much work on the farm and so much food for her and her four brothers and two sisters. There was no work in Ireland due to an economic depression which resulted in high unemployment and high emigration. Julia's primary education consisted of learning to read, write, sew, cook and pray. Because she was smart and spoke up in class she was reminded with a rap of the ruler to know her place. It did not help that she was beautiful as the nuns felt she was a distraction to boys. She finished primary school and stayed home to help her mother with her younger sisters and brothers to live a life that consisted of washing, ironing, cooking, and scrubbing floors. Julia's mother wanted more for her eldest daughter.

"Julia, I've written to Tom and he is sure he can find work for you in America."

"America, but Mam__"

"You are smart and if you stay here you'll have a life like you have now. I want more for you. I know you can do it. Tom will help you. You'll be eighteen next month time to think about your future."

Julia looked into her mother's eyes full of love and pleading.

"If you think it is right for me then I'll go."

Six weeks later, Julia had her papers in her hand and her airline ticket to her future. There was a knock on the door and Julia turned to see Mr. Hennessey walk in.

"Mornin', lass." He bowed from the waist and removed his cap. He was short and rotund. Grey whiskers covered his jowls but couldn't hide his wide grin.

"Morning, Mr. Hennessey," replied Julia.

"I hear tell the Americans pay people to cut their grass. All I have to do is let my cows do the job." His belly shook as he laughed.

"Can I offer you a cup of tea, Mr. Hennessy?" asked Julia's mother.

"Don't mind if I do."

Mr. Hennessey sipped his tea and waited for Julia's father who was to accompany them to Shannon to come in. Mr. Hennessey knew they would stop for a pint in the local pub after Julia was gone and lament the fact that young people were leaving Ireland for distant shores which promised prosperity.

Julia stood next to her suitcases with a ticket to her new life in her hand. She said goodbye and saved her mother for last. Mary wrapped her arms around Julia.

"I'll pray for you every night. You are smart and I know you will be fine. Get your rest and write as soon as you can."

"Yes, Mam."

"Remember, you can always come back home. God be with you."

"Thanks, Mam."

Shannon was crowded with young people saying goodbye to their families not knowing when they would see them again. John O'Brien said goodbye to his son, Tom, but Julia was his daughter and he hated letting her go.

"Write to us. Don't go out without Tom. Say your prayers and be good."

"I'll write as soon as I get there, Pa. Don't worry." She hugged him tight and boarded the plane.

The stewardesses were especially attentive to Julia who was taking her first plane trip to a foreign land to begin a new life. They told her that Boston was favorable to the Irish especially one as young and beautiful as she. They gave her two pillows and a blanket after dinner, turned off her light and encouraged her to sleep and if not, just to doze.

Julia felt a hand on her arm. The stewardess told her they were about to land. Julia sat up straight and looked out of the window of the plane to see the city of Boston below. A farm girl moving to the city; she extended her neck trying to take it all in. She was stepping into a new life. She reached inside her bag and moved her hand over the Irish bread her mother had given her.

When she stepped off the plane she looked around for Tom's familiar face until her eyes rested on him and she called out, "Tom, Tom." He greeted her with a hug while she babbled on for ten minutes until she noticed a man staring at them. Tom beckoned for the man to come forward.

"This is Donal, my partner. He comes from the next village in Ireland close to our family. Hope you don't mind that I asked him to come."

Julia felt her mouth go dry. She had to look up to see his dark blue eyes and black hair, partially covered by a cap and his wide grin.

"Not at all," she answered.

Gazing at Julia, Donal was speechless. They shook hands and a spark was ignited.

They had a light supper at Curran's and Donal offered to show Julia the way to her work the following Monday. From then on they were inseparable.

Julia wrote often to her family always including stories about Tom and of course Donal. She told them of her work at the

Community Center which provided immigration and naturalization technical assistance to new immigrants along with information on places to live and employment.

The staff of eight at the Community Center was overwhelmed with requests. Julia never tired of repeated questions. She would carry a suitcase for someone to one of the cubicles holding their elbow and telling them they were doing just fine and everything would be alright in a calm and reassuring voice. Occasionally one would return to learn more and they would ask for her. At the end of each day Donal met her, waiting to hear about Julia's day with "her people" as she called them.

One night, after having a meal at Curran's, Donal and Julia were sipping coffee. The usually talkative Donal was quiet as he stirred his coffee and looked at Julia then back to his coffee and then back to Julia.

"What is it, Donal?" she asked.

"We've been seeing each other a year now and...that is...Julia, will you marry me."

She laughed out loud. "Yes, yes. I will."

They were married the following month and began their life together.

Piles of multi colored leaves crunched under their feet as they walked hand in hand through the park near their house. It was brisk but not cold; the sun's warm rays shone on them through bare trees. Julia and Donal were discussing where they should go for an anniversary dinner. Julia's hand tightened on Donal's as a woman pushing a baby carriage came into their view. The woman stopped, leaned in to the carriage, smiled, and then continued walking. They parted to let the woman pass. Had there always been this many children or did she not notice them before she kept track of her periods that continued month after month?

It had only been a year since they'd been married but not getting pregnant was a constant distraction for Julia who longed for a baby. Visions of motherhood trickled into her thoughts like a small stream, shallow but persistent. Pregnancy eluded her and she had no answers as to why this was happening.

"Let's sit here." Donal pointed to a bench. "Now tell me why you squeezed my hand, although I think I know why."

Julia nodded as a ball rolled under their feet followed by a young boy who stopped in front of them. Donal reached down and rolled it back to its owner.

Julia watched as the boy retrieved the ball. A year and no baby. Donal was content to let nature take its course but nature wasn't working.

Donal placed his arm along the back of the bench. "Give it time. Look, we're enjoying ourselves. A baby will come when the time is right. Why don't we go to New York for our anniversary? See *Guys and Dolls*."

"That does sound exciting."

"Good. Now, let's have dinner."

They decided on an Italian restaurant, ordered their dinners and sat quietly until Donal cleared his throat. "This baby thing has bothered me too but I don't like to talk about it."

Julia placed her hand over his.

"We have to know if we are okay."

Donal withdrew his hand.

"Alice's daughter is pregnant."

"Oh, that's the woman at work."

"Yes." Julia said, remembering how she excused herself after Alice's news and headed to the bathroom to hide her tears.

Donal looked straight ahead tapping his fingers on the table. Their food arrived. Donal ate heartily but Julia picked at hers.

"Donal..."

"Come on, enjoy your dinner. Happy anniversary," he said as he raised his glass to Julia who did the same.

Desperate to pursue her quest for an obstetrician Julia searched the yellow pages and listened for names when conversations at work turned to pregnancies and doctors. Too embarrassed to ask, she embedded the names of those who were considered well liked in her mind and she chose one. She needed to tell Donal without causing uproar so she decided she would tell him after their sojourn to New York which was three weeks away.

Julia placed the piping hot Irish stew and scones on the table as Donal ogled the fare.

"Good play. We should do that more often," Donal said.

"Yes we should. The acting and the songs were excellent."

Not wanting to disturb the moment she held her news until they had eaten their dinner and finished cleaning up.

Donal was reading the newspaper as Julia entered the living room and sat down.

"I've found a doctor."

He made no indication he heard her.

"Did you hear what I said?" she asked.

He lowered the newspaper and nodded.

"What for?"

"I'm going to get a checkup, that's all."

"What if he finds something wrong?"

"We'll think about that after he examines me."

"Do you want me to go?"

"Not just yet. We'll talk after the visit."

Julia made the appointment for the following week. She sat on the examining table waiting for Dr. Andersen to come in.

"What seems to be the problem?"

"We've been married two years and I am not pregnant," she blurted out.

"Let's talk a little." In a methodical even tone Julia revealed her fear of not having a baby, about Donal's resistance to her getting checked, about his reluctance to even discuss the fact that she wasn't pregnant. Dr. Andersen's eyes never left Julia's face and when he did speak his voice was deep and soothing.

"I will examine you first and then we'll talk some more."

Dr. Andersen removed his gloves and Julia sat up. "I can't find anything wrong with you on examination. There is a limit as to what we can do but we can find out if your fallopian tubes are blocked. I can schedule that test for you. In the meantime, try not to think about it too much. My secretary will schedule the test and call you when she has it set up."

Julia's hope soared. Maybe there is something wrong and maybe they can fix it.

She listened intently as the doctor continued.

"There is one more thing, adoption. Some of my patients have been very successful with that."

"First I want the test done."

"Yes, but do think about adoption. There are plenty of babies out there who need parents."

Julia repeated her story to Donal that evening. He was skeptical.

"What does that test involve? Will you be okay? And why did he talk of adoption? I don't want a baby if it's not ours."

"It's just a thought. The test is simple."

"Do you need me to go with you? Because if you do I'll have to make up something to tell Tom about being out of work."

"No need, I can go by myself."

"Fine."

Julia sat facing Dr. Andersen across his desk, folding and unfolding her hands.

"Your fallopian tubes are clear, Mrs. Shea," said Dr. Andersen. "I can see no reason for you not to be able to get pregnant."

Fueled by frustration, her anger burst forth. "Why me, why me! We've been trying for two years and still no baby. No baby!" She stood, wrapped her arms around her middle and went to the window. "I want to stop thinking about it but I can't. I want to be an ordinary family with children. Why am I being denied this?"

"No one knows. These things happen. As I said earlier, there is always adoption."

Julia let this thought register as the doctor slid a pamphlet across his desk.

"It's about adoption, just think about it."

"Thank you." On the way out she murmured. "Adoption. Adoption." She placed the pamphlet in her purse and left the office.

That evening she slid the pamphlet across the dinner table to Donal who looked at it and immediately protested.

"Adoption! Never!" he roared. "Not for us. You don't know anything about these babies. Who their folks are. Where they come from."

"Other people do it and they're fine," said Julia.

"We're not other people. I want my own children not someone else's."

"What if we don't have our own children?"

"We will...we will. Give it time, Julia, give it time."

"How much time?"

"It's just that the idea bothers me."

"A baby is a baby."

"I'll feel like a failure if we do this."

"We're not failures we are two human beings who want a baby, that's all. There are other couples who have adopted babies. The doctor knows a lot of them. We can contact them and ask them about it. He'll help us."

"Well let's not tell anybody about it at least not just yet."

Julia's optimism goaded her into a frenzied search for any information she could gather on adoption. She sat with stacks of books at the library, reading about how families went about adopting babies and some who already had children of their own who had adopted. She would recite all the pertinent points to Donal each evening. His passivity grated on her.

"Donal," she shouted, slamming one of books shut, "don't you realize how important this is? We need to know everything we can about this. Do you realize how many babies there are out there that need homes?"

He threw his napkin on his plate. "All I know is you can't talk about anything else and you don't want to do anything else, just read about this adoption stuff. I'm going out."

"Donal..." Ignoring her, he put on his jacket and left. Julia folded her arms on the table and placed her head down.

"Dear God, let this be over soon."

Julia was asleep on the sofa when she felt his lips brush hers. The familiar smell and touch of him enticed her to wrap her arms around his neck and pull him towards her.

"Julia," he whispered. "I'm sorry."

"Me too," she said.

He sat on the floor next to her with his arm resting on her hip.

"Donal, I must go to see my mother."

"Good idea. It's always good to go home."

The plane landed in Shannon, Ireland. It was the first time Julia had been home since leaving four years ago. Mr. Hennessey greeted her with a welcoming smile, picked up her luggage, and drove her home, filling her in on all the news of her family and village on the way. When they arrived her mother came out and wrapped her arms around her and for the moment her cares melted away. Her mother held her hand as they entered the house, immediately the glowing turf fire warmed her heart. Everything was the same: the bench along the wall, the kettle for tea on the stove, a loaf of Irish bread on the counter. A great sense of peace overwhelmed her as she squeezed her Mother's hand. Surely her family wondered why she did not have any children. Her brothers ran to her firing questions off faster than she could answer.

"Tell us about America. Is your house big?"

"Are the Americans friendly?"

"Have you made a lot of money?"

"Now boys, give her a chance to get settled." Mary O'Brien warned her sons.

"Come, darlin', we'll have tea first," Mary said as she led Julia towards the kitchen. Ham and cabbage were simmering over the fireplace. Mary poured the tea. The door opened and her brother Robert came in with his wife, Delia, whose large abdomen preceded her. Julia's eye brows shot upward. No one had told her about the pregnancy. Julia's mother circled her waist pulling her close.

Delia approached Julia, took her hands in hers and kissed her cheek. "How nice to see you, Julia. Welcome home."

"Nice to see you too."

The family sat around the table. John O'Brien led the prayer in thanks for bringing Julia safely home and for blessing the family with the upcoming birth of the first grandchild. Holding her emotions to herself, Julia listened as they talked of names and discussed whether it was a boy or girl. When supper was over the family stood in the doorway and waved goodbye to Delia and Robert. Julia turned and went upstairs to her bedroom, seeing this her mother followed.

"Julia. Are you alright?"

"Of course, why wouldn't I be?" she answered as she unpacked.

"I haven't seen you in four years but you're my child and I can tell when something is bothering you. Is it Donal?"

Julia stuffed her clothes into a drawer. "No."

"And your job is okay?"

"It's fine."

"You've been married three years."

Julia slid her suitcase under the bed, stood, faced her mother and said evenly.

"Yes and no babies. I'm desperate."

Her mother hesitated then motioned to Julia to sit next to her on the bed.

"Julia, sometimes there are no answers to why things happen. Despair can drive happiness from your life. You're strong, you're beautiful and smart. You're still young. Have faith. God has a plan for all of us. Trust Him and trust yourself."

"Donal and I have talked of adoption," she said and waited for her mother's response.

"Ahh, you do trust yourself. Good. A baby is a baby. You'll make a fine mother."

Julia flourished during her visit. She slept soundly in her old bed, hiked through the fields in back of her family home breathing in the smell of turf. She fell under the watchful eyes of cows chewing and nuzzling their young as she pulled her mother's shawl closer around her and stared back. Reaching the highest point she sat and drew her knees up to her chest. She wondered what a baby's breath would feel like against her neck, the softness of its hair and the softness of flannel when her arms wrapped around its small body. *I will have my own baby. If it's adopted I will love it just as if it were my own.*

The week came to a close and Julia was anxious to return to Donal.

"Did you enjoy yourself, Julia?" her mother asked taking her hands in hers.

"Yes, Mam, it's always good coming here."

"You look refreshed. Must be the Irish air."

"I've had time to think and when I go home I will pursue adoption. I know it is right for us. I'm sure of it."

"Good. It will all work, you'll see."

They embraced and Julia left for Boston and Donal.

Their appointment with the adoption agency was scheduled for Tuesday. Julia pinched her cheeks to get some color in them and tried on three outfits before she chose one. She was ready by one o'clock. Breathing deeply, she waited for Donal, who arrived at two o'clock.

"Are you going to change?"

"To what? I'm the same inside even when I'm dressed up."

When they arrived at the agency Julia reminded Donal to speak in a clear voice and not too fast as he was prone to do.

"I'll be on my best behavior just like I promised."

They opened the door that had an opaque glass in the upper half with the words *Catholic Charities Adoption Agency* in bold letters affixed to it. Julia took a deep breath. The women at the desk removed her glasses, smiled and said, "May I help you?"

"We're here to see about an adoption. We have an appointment," said Donal in a clear voice and not too fast. Julia broke into a smile.

"Have a seat; Mr. Kelley will be with you shortly."

Donal and Julia sat wordlessly waiting until the door to an inner office opened and a short stout man with white hair stepped out.

"Mr. and Mrs. Shea?"

They nodded and entered the office behind Mr. Kelley. On Mr. Kelley's large desk was a folder, a pencil holder with two pencils, a telephone, a stapler and a small picture of a man and woman and three children.

When they were seated Mr. Kelly folded his hands and said.

"Now, my name is John, what can I do for you?"

Julia cleared her throat. "We're interested in adopting a baby."

Donal repositioned himself in his chair and nodded.

"I see. How long have you been married?"

"Three years."

"Have you any children or have you ever been pregnant?"

"No, no."

"Alright. Please fill out these forms and when you're done we'll talk more."

The form was three pages long and asked every detail of their lives: what their income was, what activities they liked, what church they attended, how much money they had in savings, what their social life was, did they have pets? The questions went on and on and when they were done they handed them back to John who looked them over.

"After we contact your references, if they are in order, we'll schedule a home visit. The process to adopt is lengthy and can be intimidating. I hope you understand that."

"Yes, we do. What is a home visit?" asked Julia.

"We will ask about your background, education, employment, daily life, we will inspect your home to check for safety and where the child will sleep, we'll also look at your neighborhood and the community where the child will grow up. Your life will be an open book. It takes a while but I'm sure you understand why we do this. We will be placing a baby in your care and we must be sure it is the right thing to do for the child. Will there be anything else?" John asked standing and dismissing them.

Walking to the car Donal asked Julia if she thought John ever smiled.

"Maybe in his sleep."

A month later the home visits began with Wednesday being the day the social worker would arrive. The questions asked over a period of six months covered every imaginable aspect of their lives: what is your family background, parents, siblings, what you enjoy doing, what is your educational background, what do you do for a living, do you like what you do, what is your total annual income, how do you manage your finances, what do you do for recreation?

A dusting of snow was on the ground, the sun had yet to rise. Julia dressed for the weather and left the house. Hoping to keep her tears from freezing on her face she covered the bottom of her face with a scarf. She hadn't slept well in weeks and she and Donal argued constantly.

What is there to do? We have to continue. One foot in front of the other. More tears. *We've given them everything, answered their foolish questions. Do you like this? Do you like that? Where is the baby going to sleep? I'm so tired, I can hardly get up in the morning and when I do all I can think of is a baby. Why couldn't I just get pregnant? It would have been so easy.* She turned the corner and a sharp wind hit her in the face. *By God, I'll finish this if it's the last thing I do.* A rim of the sun peeked through, she stopped and looked up. *A new year, 1957, maybe things will go our way.*

She arrived home before Donal woke and put on the coffee. He came downstairs, poured himself a cup and stared at Julia sitting at the table drinking hers.

"It can't be much longer. I can't think of anything else they need to know."

Julia looked at him. "If they do, we'll give it them."

There was no need. The following week they received a letter informing them that the home visits were finished. A panel would review the findings and they would be notified of the results as soon as they became known.

Julia crumbled the letter and sobbed with relief. When Donal arrived home he saw the letter and she told him what was in it. One step closer to adoption.

Tulips and daffodils pushed through the ground. Donal worked incessantly in the yard, even picturing where a swing set might go and maybe a sandbox. Julia saw a rocking chair in the local furniture but refused to sit in it. The wait was interminable. Mail was like gold. They sifted through it looking first at the return address in the upper left hand corner of the envelope. Then one day it came. Donal saw it and tore open the envelope.

> Dear Mr. and Mrs. Shea
> We are pleased to inform you that your application for adoption has been passed and you are now on a waiting list for a baby. Please accept our congratulations.
> You will be notified when a baby is ready for your consideration.

"Julia, Julia." Donal went running upstairs and almost fell into the shower with her.

"Look!" he waved the letter at her until it began getting wet. She stepped out wrapped herself in a towel and read the letter out loud.

The car pulled into the driveway. Donal got out followed by Julia. They opened the trunk and carefully lifted out the rocking chair and carried it upstairs to the empty room that over the next weeks would be turned into a nursery. Then they waited again. Labor Day weekend arrived and Tom arrived for supper.

"Have you heard anything about our baby?"

"He'll have two fathers," laughed Donal.

"What do you mean 'he'? It might be a girl," said Julia.

"If it's a boy Peter sounds like a good name," said Donal.

"If it's a girl how about Hannah?" said Julia.

"A toast to Peter or Hannah and may they arrive soon," said Tom.

Donal and Julia took their daily walk through the park near their house. When baby carriages passed they commented on how nice the carriages were and compared them to the one they'd purchased. They decided to have dinner at the same Italian restaurant.

"Order for me, Donal, I'm too excited to think!"

"We thought this day would never come and here we are. We're going to be parents at last. I don't mind telling you I always thought we would."

Julia arched her eyebrows and glared.

The next morning the telephone rang, Julia answered. "Hello."

"Mrs. Shea?"

"Yes."

"This is Ann Marie Hale at the adoption agency."

Julia caught her breath and sat down.

"Yes, Ann Marie."

"We have a baby for you and Mr. Shea. He was born September 2. We set a date for you and your husband to come in on October 14 at nine o'clock to sign the initial adoption papers. The final adoption will take place in court in six months. Is that date alright?"

"Yes, yes. Oh, yes. Of course we'll be there."

Julia called Donal.

"It's a boy and he's waiting for us! Peter is waiting for us!"

Chapter Nine

⁓

It had been three weeks since Peter's adoption. Julia nuzzled him close to her, planted her lips on his soft, downy cheeks and murmured sounds into his tiny ears while Peter tried to suck on Julia's chin. Donal would doze on the couch full length with Peter lying on top of him, both covered by the hand knitted shawl from Julia's mother. Julia sipped her tea and watched the contented pair.

I don't see how I could love a baby more even if I gave birth to it. I can't imagine giving a baby to strangers but his mother must have been ill or maybe was forced to give him up. I thank her every day for giving us Peter.

When Peter sat up by himself and did not fall over, Julia thought he was the most amazing baby. Undaunted by the fact that he would fall down he mastered the art of walking by walking all over the house planting his bare feet firmly on the floor. Julia was sure he was exceptional. They read books, put puzzles together, and he would scrawl pictures on construction paper which Julia hung in the kitchen. Peter belonged to Julia in every way. She loved him dearly.

Peter handed Julia the toy he had in his hand. He was two now and shared his possessions with mamma. When Donal arrived home he would call Peter's name. Peter dropped what he was doing and scamper to the door where Donal would whisk him in the air.

During outings Peter would wave to people passing by, say hi to anyone he came across and would carry on a conversation with those who would listen. If his playmates cried he would stop and watch while their mothers soothed them and then he would continue playing

"Donal, Donal," Julia called as she entered the house. "Where are you?"

"I'm here in the bathroom trying to fix a faucet."

Julia ran upstairs and blurted out. "I'm pregnant."

Donal stood with the wrench in his hand. "What? Pregnant! How…"

"That's right, just came from a doctor's visit. Can you believe it? It was my usual checkup and I don't pay attention to my periods that much and there it was. Doctor Andersen was as excited as I was."

Donal dropped the wrench and grabbed Julia hugging her close. Peter would have a sibling. It was more than they could hope for.

Julia and Donal knew the time had come to discuss adoption with Peter, who was almost three years old. How would they start the conversation with him and how would they answer questions that he surely would have? They decided to tell him about the baby first, this would lead into how he was born.

One night while they were eating dinner, Julia began…

"Peter, Daddy and I have something to tell you." She looked at her blue eyed little boy with light brown hair who was already showing signs of an inquisitive mind asking where the sun goes at night and how the stars stay up in the sky.

Peter looked at his mother his face filled with wonder.

"You are going to have a baby sister or brother."

"I am," he said.

"You know, Peter, when mommy and I got you we adopted you. Adoption means parents chose a baby, which means we chose you."

Peter looked at his father. "How did you do that?"

"We contacted people who know how to find babies."

"Are they lost?"

"No, but some parents can't take care of babies and these people know who they are."

"Are you going to adopt this baby?"

"No it's going to grow in mommy's stomach."

Peter was wide eyed. "It is!"

"Yes," answered Julia.

"Did I grow in your stomach?"

"No, we chose you but you grew in someone else's stomach."

"I did!"

"Yes, you did," answered Julia.

"Is she my mommy too?"

"Yes," said Julia.

"So I have two mommies."

"That's right," said Donal.

"Do you know where my other mommy is?"

"No, Peter. We don't. Now then, let's finish our supper."

Six months later Julia delivered a healthy baby girl, whom they named Hannah. Julia brushed her mouth against the baby's soft cheeks and stroked her head still damp from birth fluids, thinking again how heart wrenching it must have been for Peter's mother to give him up.

The love Donal and Julia showered on Hannah was equal to the love they showered on Peter. They were a family unit created by marriage, adoption and blood.

Peter was amazed at this new baby, how tiny she was and how his mother had to do so much for her. He would show her pictures in his books and share his trucks with her. He asked Julia how the baby would tell her what she wanted if she couldn't talk. Julia explained that's why babies cry, they need something. Peter was astonished more than ever about his little sister. He watched as she took her first steps and graduated from a crib to a bed.

Peter looked forward to entering school in the fall. Every day he would ask Julia how long he had to wait before he could go.

"Have patience, Peter, it will come, besides, I will miss you when you go," she said hugging him.

The first day of school Peter stood next to a tall thin boy with black hair and a dimpled chin waiting to go into the building. He looked directly at Peter and said. "My name is Richard, what's yours?"

"Peter."

Peter told Richard he was adopted and Richard told Peter that he was not.

Their friendship started that day and continued beyond the classroom, playing ball in Peter's back yard, racing trucks, taking swimming lessons at the local YMCA and riding their bikes to baseball practice with Peter always in the lead.

Ever since the word adoption entered into his vocabulary, Peter was curious. They choose him. Did his other mother just go away? He knew his parents loved him. Their warm embraces, their encouraging words. They seemed really happy when Hannah was growing inside his mother's stomach but he wondered if his mother was happy when he grew inside hers.

It was June, Julia was in the garden and Peter and Hannah were helping her plant tomatoes.

"Mom, where was I born?"

"In Boston. Why do you ask?" She sat back on her heels looking at Peter.

"Well, I just thought maybe my mother still lives where I was born."

"I don't know where she lives, sweetheart. I don't know anything about her," she said wrapping her arms around him.

"Who does?" he asked.

"Why do you want to know?"

"You have Mommy, Peter," said Hannah.

"I know but I'd like to know where she lives."

"Peter, when Daddy and I adopted you we did it through an agency that handles adoptions. Your father and I were so happy and loved you from the moment we laid eyes on you. Maybe they have information on her and maybe they don't," she said holding Peter's hands. Peter turned and continued digging.

One afternoon the boys were eating hot dogs in Peter's backyard when Richard asked Peter what being adopted was like.

Peter shrugged his shoulders. "It's no different than having a real mother and father. They treat Hannah and me the same."

"Do you know where your real mother is?"

Peter shook his head.

"Did you ever see her?'

"No."

"Do you know where she lives?"

"No, but someday I'm going to find her."

"You are!"

"Yes."

"I'll help you find her."

"You will?"

"Sure, I love detective work."

The boys finished their hot dogs and starting throwing a baseball to each other.

One night, just before going to bed, Peter told Julia that Richard was going to help him find his real mother. Julia passed this off to Peter's highly imaginative nature and simply said it was a good idea. Peter academic excellence was beginning to show, his love of books and figuring out how things work was astonishing to Julia and Donal and his teachers.

It was a warm spring day with bright sun reminding Julia of Ireland. Thirteen year old Peter and ten year old Hannah left for school. Julia waved as they boarded the school bus.

Standing on the sidewalk she waited until the bus was no longer in her view. *How the years go by. I must go back to Ireland, maybe this summer with Peter and Hannah. Peter will be going to high school in the fall. He has grown so tall.*

She tried to answer his questions about his mother but she didn't have much information; all she remembered was that she signed the adoption papers and was given an envelope which she never opened and was unaware of where it was or what was inside, maybe Donal will remember. When Donal came home she would ask him about the envelope, she was sure he would remember where it was.

She walked back to the house feeling adrift. Lately she couldn't seem to concentrate on one thing. She thought she must see about these nagging headaches she had been having. She stopped at the garden to check on her vegetables, pulled some weeds and when the basket was full, she headed back to the house. She climbed the stairs leading to the back door, placed the basket on the top step and opened the door. Her hand shook but she grasped the knob, turned it and pulled it open.

This dull headache is a nuisance and that dizzy spell this morning was upsetting. I must see about it soon.

She walked into the kitchen, removed her gardening gloves, placed them on the table and slid to the floor.

That afternoon when Donal arrived home he walked in and found Julia's lifeless body on the floor. He screamed, "Julia!" and lifted her body to a sitting position. "Julia, wake up, please. Oh dear God wake her up. Julia, don't leave us. Wake up, wake up!" He shook her and then cradled her in his arms trying to breathe life back into her. He rocked her back and forth tears spilling out of his eyes.

He stopped and looked at her face, which was drained of color, "Julia."

Her lips were blue and her eyes were half closed, her flaccid arms hung loose at her side.

Panicking, Donal released his wife's body, flew to the phone and with shaking hands he dialed the operator and demanded an ambulance, almost forgetting what his address was. He then began his wait. Donal heard the sirens and held on to his last thread of hope that his Julia would live.

Donal followed the ambulance to the hospital and when he was sure Julia was in the hands of professionals he called Tom, asked him to meet the children after school and told him why.

Donal paced back and forth in the emergency room waiting for news, hoping someone would come to tell him that his wife would survive, until a doctor walked out of Julia's room with a grim look on his face.

"I'm sorry..." Donal didn't hear the rest he collapsed in a heap hearing muted voices around him. "Poor man." "She was so young." "Let's get him a place to lie down."

A few minutes later Donal's eyes opened and sitting in a chair next to him was an orderly holding a glass of water which he offered to Donal. After taking a sip, reality seized Donal's mind and he cried out. "Julia."

Julia died of a brain tumor. She was thirty six years old. Donal felt totally detached from his surroundings as he signed the necessary papers. He forgot where he parked his car and while wandering around in a dreamlike state he found it. As he entered, on the passenger seat was Julia's scarf. He buried his face in it and sobbed. His next task was to tell Peter and Hannah their mother was dead.

Peter and Hannah saw Tom's truck in the driveway and sprinted up the stairs into the house.

"Tom," Peter called out. "What are you doing here? Where's Mom?"

Donal pulled into the driveway, jumped out of the car, ran to the front door pushed it open and when Peter saw his reddened eyes and the look of utter disbelief on his father's face, fear crept into Peter's body.

"What is it? Where's Mom?" cried Peter.

Feeling something bad happened Hannah started to scream.

"Mommy, where's Mommy?"

"She's gone."

"Gone! Gone where?" cried Hannah.

"She's dead. She's dead," Donal shook his head from side to side.

Hannah started to scream again, Peter held her and Donal wrapped his arms around his children, trying to sooth them, trying to make the hurt go away but his own hurt got in the way of him being able to do so. Peter's mind escalated. *It can't be, she just saw us off to school, there must be a mistake, she wasn't sick, she wasn't old...it can't be.* But the look on his father's face told him it was true, his mother was dead.

A cloud settled over the household, which could not be moved by sun or blue skies. Life as they knew it came to an abrupt halt. Peter was numb since being told his mother was dead. He said little, ate little and spent most of his time on the back porch. Tom, who had moved in to help out, would bring him a sandwich which Peter would accept and then toss it in the garbage. Julia's Mother, who came over from Ireland, would come out on the porch trying to engage Peter in conversation.

"I'm not in the mood to talk and if you don't mind I'd rather be alone."

"It's okay, son, I understand."

"No, you don't."

Mary O'Brien reached out to Peter and he shrank from her gesture.

"You lost your mother and I lost a daughter but maybe we can help each other go on without her." Mary said softly.

Julia's funeral was dark and somber, prayers were said, audible sobs could be heard and at the cemetery people offered their condolences in low murmurs. Donal, Peter and Hannah fell under the watchful eye of Tom who held his grief close. Mary O'Brien wondered how she could bind their wounds and ease their loss as well as her own.

Peter went to his bedroom, closed the door, kicked off his shoes and sat on the edge of the bed. Tears came slowly at first then a small stream that clouded his eyes, his shoulders shook and his grip tightened on the bedspread. The sadness and loss he felt was deep inside in a place that peace and hope could not find. His body dropped to one side, his legs automatically lifted onto the bed. He felt powerless. The sobbing continued. The knife like pain of loss was as sharp as a razor's edge.

The door opened; a shaft of light from the hallway entered along with Donal.

"Peter, Peter. Are you alright? I came to say goodnight," Donal said as he approached the bed.

His face red and swollen, Peter looked at his father, "Dad, I've lost another Mother!"

Donal reached out to hold him, and they began to sway back and forth. In an instant they became one in sadness and loss and one in hope and peace. Donal left the room when Peter fell asleep.

Three weeks later the family gathered in the living room. Peter and Hannah were seated on the couch with Tom. Mary O'Brien was sitting in a chair opposite the couch. Donal sat on the arm of Mary's chair facing his children.

"Peter, Hannah," Donal began, "we've had a terrible loss but we must go on as Mom would want us to. Do you understand?"

"What does that mean, Dad?" asked Peter.

"You and Hannah are going to live in Ireland with your grandparents until I can sort things out here."

"Ireland! But we've always lived here," shouted Peter as he jumped off the couch.

"Ireland is the country of our ancestors."

"I have no ancestors!" said Peter.

The following day Peter asked Donal if he could spend his last night with Richard and Donal agreed. The two boys who had been inseparable since first grade were saying their goodbyes not knowing when or if they would they would see each other again. Richard was now an inch taller than Peter, a fact that he teased Peter with asking him to catch up.

"We'll write, won't we?" asked Richard.

Peter nodded. He felt like he was dangling a ten pound weight from each hand.

"Richard—" Peter began.

"It's okay, Peter. Maybe you can come here for a visit next summer and stay with us or with your Uncle Tom."

Again Peter nodded but this time with a thin smile.

"We'll start the search for your mother."

Peter glanced up at his friend tears welling up.

"We will. We will," he said.

"You'll have a lot of cousins in Ireland. Your mother has a big family."

"They're not really my cousins, though."

"Maybe not but I bet they're fun."

Richard's parents allowed them to stay up as long as they liked and extended an invitation to Peter to come visit whenever he wanted.

The next day Donal arrived with Hannah and Mary. Peter climbed into the back seat and watched Richard's figure diminish until they turned the corner and headed to Logan Airport. The fact that Peter was taking his first air plane ride did not distract from his anxiety about the move and being without his father. Would he ever be happy again? He doubted it.

Saying goodbye to his father was almost as heart wrenching as losing his mother.

"You'll come soon, Dad."

"I will, I promise. As soon as I sort things out with Tom who has agreed to buy the house and business. Take care of yourself and Hannah."

Once they boarded the plane, had dinner and darkness arrived, Mary O'Brien placed pillows behind her grandchildren's head, covered them with a blanket and lay her hand across their lap for their journey. She prayed for them and her family and for the soul of her daughter, Julia, before dozing off.

Donal got back in his car after seeing them off, sat in the driver's seat and stared straight ahead. Out loud he said, "Julia, Julia, help me." At that point he heard a tap on the window. He looked and saw a security guard.

"Are you okay, mister? You look like you've lost your best friend."

"I did," Donal replied.

"I know how you feel. I lost mine too. But she's around checking up on me to be sure I'm doing the right thing," he said pointing with his finger to the sky.

Within two months Donal sold his share of the business and his house to Tom and moved to Ireland. He looked forward to moving back home and being with his children. Julia was making sure he did the right thing, or so it seemed at the time.

Chapter Ten

❧

Julia's brother, Dennis, picked up the weary travelers at Shannon and grabbed two pieces of luggage in each hand. His brown hair curled around the edges of his black cap which he wore low over his forehead. Peter and Hannah clung to each other. Their grandmother, who was longing for relief from sadness, was glad to be home.

"Well, what have we here? Two fine looking children. Welcome, the family is waiting to meet you," said Dennis.

Peter and Hannah looked at each other and grinned.

"How are things here?" asked Mary.

"Getting bad, Mam. Lots of disturbances in Northern Ireland and people are coming here for refuge against the fighting. Don't know where or how it will end," he answered in a deep voice.

"We'll stay out of it, son, we have a farm to run, a family and Julia's children to care for."

"Too late, Mam, while you were gone Billy left with Sean O'Keefe to help out. They left before dawn last Tuesday and there's no word since."

"God help us! Is there any way of finding out if they are alright? My Billy is only nineteen years old." Mary O'Brien blanched, blessed herself and said, "I've lost a daughter, I will not lose any more of my children at least if I can help it."

"Maybe I can get the word out, but it's tough, Ma."

Peter listened. *What is the disturbance, where was the north and why is my grandmother worried? Must be some kind of trouble.*

The brood of O'Briens welcomed Peter and Hannah with sympathy on their loss and said how glad they were to have them here with their family. Peter watched with interest as John O'Brien motioned his sons to follow him out to the barn. Julia's sisters prepared a breakfast of oatmeal, eggs, ham, tomatoes, brown bread and plenty of hot tea for their guests which they ate heartily. Peter carried his luggage to the room he would share with Dennis, unpacked, and laid down on top of the bed covers and was soon fast asleep until he was wakened by Hannah who shook him vigorously.

"Peter, wake up. Come downstairs supper's ready. You slept all day. Aunt Erin showed me all around the farm, they have lots of cows and sheep and dogs round them up. She said I could milk a cow. Come on wake up. There's all kinds of food being cooked."

Peter opened his eyes and looked at Hannah, all he could see was his mother, she looked so like her, red hair, blue eyes, freckles, fair skin and a beautiful smile; by contrast he was not as fair as she with brown hair and blue eyes and one freckle on the back of his left arm.

He sat up and threw his legs over the side of the bed and remembered where he was and why. He hung his head down wishing for more sleep to avoid the loss that gripped his heart but he knew he must go on and reluctantly allowed Hannah to pull him by the hand downstairs to their new life.

The following week Peter entered the ninth grade. He woke that morning with a sense of dread that could not be relieved. He thought of Richard and the hopes they had of being in the same class starting high school together. Mary O'Brien walked him to school, telling him to study hard and there was no problem that could not be fixed. All he needed to do is to tell her and she would see to it. Erin walked Hannah to school and introduced Hannah to several children taking the same path.

Mary O'Brien introduced Peter to the principal who merely shook Peter's hand, said goodbye to Mary and walked Peter to his classroom. Peter was taller than most boys in the class which made him stand out, or so he felt. At the end of the school day Peter was the first one out of school. He walked home as fast as he could and headed to his room for solace. The ache in his stomach remained.

It was the end of Peter's first full week at school and things were not going well. The work was confusing; it was hard to understand the teacher and some of his classmates. He ate lunch alone and no one seemed to take any notice of him, it was getting unbearable and he was yet to hit a baseball. Feeling quite rejected he left school immediately when classes were over and headed home. Half way there he was approached by three boys he did not recognize. They surrounded him.

"Hey Yank, where's your Ma and Pa?"

"He don't have any," said the other.

Peter walked away trying to avoid a confrontation; he was unsuccessful as one of the boys blocked his way.

"I asked you something."

"None of your business," said Peter.

The boy shoved Peter, Peter recovered and shoved him back when a second boy grabbed Peter's arms and held him as a fist landed on the side of his face and the last thing Peter heard before he fell was a crack in his jaw. When he opened his eyes a boy with black hair, dark eyes, a round face and a determined look on his face was kneeling next to him.

"That was those thugs from across the other side of the village. They're bad news. I saw them come after you but didn't make it in time. Are you alright? Can you stand? Your face looks pretty bad."

"Yes, I'm okay.

"Name's Connor, Connor Murphy."

"I'm Peter Shea, I'm living with my___"

"I know who you are. My pa knew your mother. Said she was fine lass, a real beauty and a big loss for your family. Let's get you home. You better have your jaw looked after."

"Your family knew her?"

"Yes, she grew up near us. Pa said your family is nice people."

"Do you know that I was adopted?"

"I do."

"I guess word gets around."

"The people here care about each other. They like knowing each other's stories, know what I mean? The Irish think if you know a person's story you can understand them better."

"I don't have my full story yet," said Peter.

"Don't matter. It's what you feel in here," Connor said pointing to his heart. "I've seen you in school but you always disappeared after and I figured you wanted it that way."

"I did. I miss my friends."

"Well, you'll have to get new ones and you can start with me. We're at your house; wait till your grandmother sees you."

Mary O'Brien was the first to see Peter and ordered her son Dennis to bring the car around and drive Peter to the hospital. Two hours later Peter returned with a massive bandage on the side of his face covering most of his bruised skin and with a warning to stay away from bad characters. Connor would make sure of that.

That night, sleep eluded Peter. Visions of the thugs haunted him. Would they attack him again? Would he be lucky to get away with only a bruised chin? If they stayed in Boston would this have happened? He thought not. For the first time in his life he felt fear which he added to the loss, sadness and loneliness he felt.

The following morning at his grandmother's insistence Peter stayed home from school. He was only too glad to do so. Mary O'Brien made him soup and tea, insisting he rest, calling his attackers shameful and ruffians.

The next day when Peter returned to school, he noticed many boys smiling at him and nodding. He was joined at the lunch table by six boys who introduced themselves. Connor and Peter walked home together after school.

"I see you had company at lunch."

"Yeah. They seem okay."

"The shove helped. They admire you for standing up to the thugs."

Peter laughed and rubbed his sore jaw.

Connor and Peter spent afternoons kicking a soccer ball or watching television at Connor's house on one of the three channels available and even those broke down often. They studied together and Connor helped Peter understand the Irish education system. On the weekend they hopped on the buses which were open in the back where they could jump on and off in between stops. In the months that followed Peter began to feel more Irish than American. He no longer ate alone in school; he understood his teachers better and was included in any sports.

Peter wrote to Richard at Christmas time and received a lengthy reply about baseball, his classes in high school, the pretty girl he sat next to in school named, Nancy and how he missed Peter.

With the arrival of Donal, the family was reunited and Peter's anxiety adjusting to a new place and a new school was lessened, especially when they moved to a small house which Donal purchased near the O'Briens and began their life together without Julia.

At breakfast one morning Donal explained to Peter and Hannah about the trouble in the Northern Ireland.

"It is a territorial conflict bought on by discrimination against Catholics in Northern Ireland and the inability to solve political and social conflict by the unionists who dominated Northern Ireland parliament for over fifty years and who wanted to remain part of the United Kingdom in contrast to the Nationalist and Republican minority, almost exclusively Catholic, whose goal was to become part of the Republic of Ireland. This will be a long struggle." Donal told Peter and Hannah. "It won't affect us but it may affect people we know, for instance Billy O'Brien has not been heard from in months and his family grieves for him. They lost Julia and I hope they won't have to suffer another loss. We'll have to wait and see."

The dampness and cold bought on by the Irish winters permeated the household and was made bearable for Peter by woolen sweaters, hot tea and a turf fire. Every evening he, Hannah and Donal would sit in front of the fire and discuss current issues, books, or whatever came into their minds. Julia was almost always remembered and Peter would broach the subject of his birth mother which usually met with silence on Donal's and Hannah's part. Who was she? Was she a good person? Does she have a family? No one could answer these questions.

Spring in Ireland meant soccer. At the insistence of Connor, Peter joined and became quite good at it even with the good natured teasing from his teammates at being an outsider.

Hannah's resemblance to members of Julia's family was a constant reminder to Peter that he was not connected to them, at least in a physical way. Hannah was tall like Erin. Often he would mention this to Hannah who would admonish him.

"What difference does it make? It's not the same without Mom but we have each other and Mom's family. What else do we need? Please stop thinking and worrying. Do you think about our mother, Peter? Because I do. I remember her softness when she held me and her smell."

"I remember her voice. Clear with a lilt. And her red hair just like yours. I will always miss her."

"Me too. At least you have another one."

"Someday, I'll find her."

Hannah shook her head and let out a long sigh.

Coming out of a sound sleep Peter heard his bedroom door open just slightly enough to realize someone was standing there. In an instant he knew...Connor.

"Come on you can't sleep all day. We've a game at noon and we better kick the ball around first." Connor pushed the curtains aside to allow the sun to stream into the room. Peter was getting used to these unannounced visits when Connor would burst through the front door calling his friend's name. Peter's fondness for Connor grew each day. Sports united Peter and Connor, their enthusiasm for anything with a ball to catch, throw or kick was matched by their abilities to play. The next Christmas Peter and Richard exchanged letters again; distance and time had not diminished their friendship.

Peter's daily strolls through the fields invigorated him. He held his head high, breathed in the fresh air, swung his arms and placed his footsteps firmly on the grass often accompanied by one or two of the dogs from his grandparent's farm. Tragedy was about to happen to the O'Brien family once again. They received notice that their son Billy was killed by gunfire in Northern Ireland, a senseless loss and one felt by the whole village as they wondered how many more people would be killed.

Discussion in Peter's history classes invariably turned most notably to the trouble in Northern Ireland and the war in Vietnam. Peter knew first-hand what senseless killing did to his grandparents and vowed never to support a cause unless it was done by peaceful means. The class agreed and disagreed with this philosophy until they had a debate during which lively points of view and heated discussion took place. Peter sharpened his listening skills which gave him a better understanding of motives and beliefs of other people. He and Connor covered many subjects during their own discussions as they headed into the third year of secondary school. Peter's grades were exceptional as were his standing with classmates and teachers. Connor would tease Peter that it was the "shove" that did it. At the end of the school year Peter's math teacher asked if he could have a word with him.

"Peter, do you have plans for further study?"

"Yes, I'm not sure where but I'm certain I want to go to college."

"You have the general requirements necessary for admission to Trinity College in Dublin."

"I never thought of Trinity."

"I think you stand a good chance for admission and I would be more than glad to write a letter of recommendation for you. They require a lot of their students but should you get accepted it will be an experience you won't forget."

"Thank you Mr. Curran. I would be most grateful."

"We best start the process. How about next week, Monday, at four o'clock in my office? I have the paper work all ready for you to fill out."

Peter shook Mr. Curran's hand with both of his and ran all the way home to tell Donal.

Donal was delighted, wondering who Peter's exceptional mind, his outgoing personality, and friendly manner came from his mother, father or both. *Trinity College, indeed. His parents would be most pleased.*

One morning when Peter was having tea at his grandparent's house, two of his uncles appeared in the kitchen and refused tea. They stood together, shifting from one foot to the other and took turns looking out of the window. Within minutes a car pulled up and the brothers left without a word. Mary O'Brien heard the car and ran from the barn to see her two sons jump in and drive away; she called their names as Peter arrived beside her.

"What is it?" Peter asked.

"They're going north to avenge their brother's death. God help us all." She blessed herself and Peter put his arms around her trying to console her.

In the weeks that followed Peter watched as his grandmother's face filled with sadness. She hardly spoke to anyone, just moved about fingering her rosary beads and uttering soft sounds. Death was about to claim another member of Peter's family, his grandmother, the glue that held the O'Brien family together, died. Once again, the shroud of grief cast a net over them. Mary O'Brien was buried in a family cemetery on their land, next to her parents. Mary O'Brien had filled the vacancy in Peter's heart for his mother and now she was gone. Peter knew sadness and it revisited him but this time he saw a resolution; if he did get accepted to Trinity, he would wait a year and help his grandfather on the farm.

"Absolutely not," said John O'Brien. "One of our own at Trinity! You wait, son, they want you and you must go. Your grandmother and your mother would want this. Robert and Delia have agreed to move back home and help out, so not another word. In the meantime, the cows have to come in. Go round up the dogs."

That spring, memories of Boston and Julia crept into Peter's mind. The house, the school he attended and the park all made up the landscape of his early years and he longed to see it again. A graduation present from Donal was a round trip plane ticket to Boston.

"How did you know this is what I wanted, Dad?"

"I just figured it was time for you to go back and have a look at things."

Instantly, Peter wrote to Tom and Richard with the news he would be coming for a visit. Peter's excitement was mixed with a tinge of sadness over what happened there.

The last four years had changed him. He grew three inches, his hair darkened, his shoulders were broader and muscle took over fat. Time spent in Ireland with his family was irreplaceable but as soon as he stepped off the plane and spotted Tom and Richard, he felt like he was home. The house was as he remembered it, but Julia's garden was gone and in its place was grass. The clothesline was gone but there was a beautiful rose bush blooming just near the back steps. Tom explained that roses were Julia's favorite and every June he placed some on her gravesite. Peter climbed the stairs to his old bedroom. It was just as he left it, nothing had changed; same curtains, same bed spread, same rug. The range of emotions from joy to sorrow filled his heart. Tom appeared at the doorway.

"You okay?"

"Yes, I am, Tom, yes I am."

Richard spent the night and they talked until daylight when they heard Tom's truck pull out of the driveway. The young men slept until noon that day. Over cereal and juice Richard asked Peter about his birth mother and his intent to find her.

"It's still there. I could spend a summer here and maybe get started but I don't even know where to begin. I've applied to Trinity College and I should be hearing from them soon. My teacher said I had a good chance of getting in. Can you imagine! So that is my first priority, then my mother."

"That is supposed to be quite the place and hard to get into. I've applied to a couple of places too."

"In Boston, I assume."

"Yeah. Lots of young people and great schools."

"Good. Anyway who is this pretty girl you told me about? Does she have a friend? Fix me up. I've got two weeks."

"I'll call her right now and see what we can do. The Northern Ireland thing is in all the papers. What do you know about it?" asked Richard as he looked up Nancy's telephone number.

"The Catholics continue to be discriminated against and the IRA is getting fierce about retribution at any costs. My uncle was killed and his two brothers went to avenge his death. We haven't heard anything about them. It killed my grandmother. She was like a Mother to me. War affects those at home too. The families in the south of Ireland do not want their sons to be killed. I'm not interested in killing or being killed but I can understand their fervor over what is happening there."

"Viet Nam is tough too. Extremes on either side."

"In the end all that is left is families torn apart and burying their dead."

The week came to an abrupt end and Peter was sorry to leave Richard but they were certain they would see each other again; even an ocean couldn't keep them apart.

"Write when you can," Peter said.

"I will and you too. Next time we'll do something to start the search for your mother."

"Maybe my dad knows something. I must have adoption papers."

They parted ways with a handshake and a shoulder pat.

"Good luck with Trinity."

"Thanks. Good luck to you, too."

Donal, Hannah and Connor picked Peter up at the airport. The sun shone bright, a perfect welcome for Peter.

"Why the entourage?" Peter asked.

Donal gave Peter a letter, the return address was from Trinity College.

"We all want to witness the news, good or bad and couldn't wait until we were home," said Donal.

Peter tore open the letter and read. He let out a yell that could have only meant one thing; he was one his way to Trinity College.

Connor arrived at the Shea's the night before Peter was to leave for Trinity. He knocked once and let himself in. Hannah already had her sweater on, Peter was finishing off his tea and Donal, who was in front of the fireplace smoking his pipe, said he would wait up for them to return.

It was a beautiful September night and a full moon lit up the sky as the three of them walked to Donovan's.

"My friend, Richard, in America said he would help me find my birth mother."

"Can we talk about something else?" asked Hannah.

"What would you like to talk about, little sister?" teased Peter.

"Like me having the house to myself after my big brother goes to college."

"Ah, you'll miss me," said Peter.

"I certainly won't," was Hannah's reply.

"How come you're always thinking about things?" Connor asked.

"You forgot the debates in school and all the discussions about life you and I had! Maybe being adopted has something to do with it. I need to know my roots."

Connor admired his friend's candor. Hannah felt uneasy because she had no idea what to expect if Peter did find his mother. She was beginning to understand his need but she still worried that he would get hurt.

"How does your father feel about it?"

"He knows I've always been interested in finding her."

"But that doesn't mean he wants you to look for her," said Hannah.

"He never said that," answered Peter.

"Suppose she doesn't want to see you? What then?" asked Connor.

"Yes. Suppose she has a family and they don't know about you," said Hannah.

"At any rate, it's Trinity first and then the search."

At the bar, Peter and Connor ordered a pint and Hannah ordered a soda as they continued their conversation.

"Connor, you know your roots. Your family goes way back in Ireland, where they lived, how they farmed the land. I don't have that. I live here but I have no history and history is important to the Irish. I feel Irish but maybe I'm not. If I find her at least I'll know my roots. Knowing is better than not knowing. But for now going to Trinity is utmost in my mind," said Peter.

The next morning Peter, Donal and Hannah walked out to the car. Hannah gave Peter one last hug and wished him well. She stood outside the house until she could no longer see the car and then headed for school. *Trinity College, our mother would be proud as would his birth mother who ever she is.*

Chapter Eleven

❦

Donal parked the car. He and Peter got out and stood on Parliament Square looking across the street at a row of buildings framed by the Public Theater on the left, the chapel on the right and in the middle was Regent House with its arch leading to the front gate of Trinity College in Dublin. Peter was choked with emotion, he had obstacles and help, hurt and healing in his young life and now he was to undertake another chapter.

City life for Peter was overwhelming, fun, exciting and exhilarating. People seemed in a hurry to get somewhere. His professors were strict and expected undivided attention in class which Peter was only too happy to give. He hung on every word spoken, his textbooks were sacred, and discourse in class was almost as good as the lectures. Thoughts of home would sneak up on him, but the excitement of Trinity and the city of Dublin nurtured him in other ways. He wrote home weekly and managed to get one letter to Richard, who had chosen Boston University.

Connor's family farm was inbred in him and he joined his father milking cows, shearing sheep and assisting animals to bring their young into the world, sun up to sundown; he could think of no other way of life. It was as natural to him as breathing.

Peter finished the year at the top of his class and headed home, this time by bus. Hannah and Donal listened as Peter talked about his classes, life in the city and his friends. He spent the summer working on his grandfather's farm, milking cows, herding them in from the fields, collecting eggs and digging potatoes. Occasionally, he and Connor would meet at Donovan's for a pint and good conversation. His second year at Trinity was fast approaching and he was anxious to return but not before he paid a visit to Mr. Curran.

Mr. Curran heard the good news but did not let on that he knew of Peter's grades.

"Come in, Peter. Well, how was your first year."

"Amazing. I got top in the class and I have you to thank."

"You're the one that did it, I just wrote the letter. Have you met any friends?"

"I've made a few friends but not like Connor and my friend from Boston. The students are mostly from wealthy families and sometime I feel out of place. I don't have the pocket money they do."

"All that matters is that you enjoy your years and use your talent. Thanks for coming by and come see anytime. Good luck next year."

I wonder who both my parents were. Were they both smart? Learning comes easy to me. Where do I get it from? Next summer I'll visit Richard and see what Tom has to say about my adoption.

Strolling through the village Peter saw a book store and decided to have a look; maybe he would find some information about adoption. As he entered a bell clanged, to his left was a table with paperback books for sale at half price, just ahead was a counter without a sales person, three bookshelves, ceiling to floor held the full inventory of the store. He spotted a ladder just behind the counter and his eyes followed it to the top where a young woman was placing books on the top shelf.

"How will anyone see those books way up there," he shouted.

The young woman glanced down and answered. "These are rare books and not for sale, only university people use them for reference. That's how much you know."

Peter laughed. He removed his black cap, set his bag down and waited for the woman to come to the counter.

She finished her task climbed down the ladder and walked over to Peter.

"Now then, what can I do for you?"

"I'm looking for books on adoption."

"Adoption?"

"Yes."

"We only have a small selection. Are you looking for anything in particular?" she asked.

"No."

"Right this way, follow me."

Peter raised his eyebrows and felt a tingle as he watched the woman walk away; her tight fitting jeans were partially covered by a loose blue knit sweater. She wore sandals on her feet. He stayed close behind the woman inhaling a scent so pleasing he became distracted and when she turned to direct him to the shelf he almost knocked her down.

"I am so sorry. It's just that..."

"That what?" she asked tossing her long brown hair off her shoulder.

"I wasn't paying attention."

"Well, you owe me a coffee for that. Now help yourself and I'll see you at the register."

Peter found four books none of which suited him. Most of the books were written about how to adopt, assistance with adoption and exploring adoption and most books were written with the adoptive parents in mind not the birth mother. The books would tell Peter how but not why. He chose two thinking he may come across some reference to the birth mother and headed for the counter where the woman waited for him.

"The name is Ellen, Ellen Adams. I'll meet you at eight here at the store," she said as she rang up his purchases.

"Right".

Peter opened the front door to his house and called to his father. Donal's voice yelled out from the kitchen. "I'm in the kitchen."

They embraced and Donal patted Peter's back.

"What have you there?" asked Donal.

"A couple of books on adoption. Don't worry Dad, first Trinity then the search. Having coffee with the girl that works there."

"Oh yes, the Adams family owns it. Moved here from Australia by way of London."

"I'm going up to my room to pack and read for a while. Be down shortly."

The next morning Peter arrived on time and saw Ellen waving at him.

"Let's go to the corner coffee shop. They have great scones," suggested Ellen.

They chose a seat by the window that had room for only a small table and two chairs.

"How come you bought books on adoption?" Ellen asked.

Peter unfolded his tale from the beginning watching rain give way to sun while nibbling at his scone and sipping his coffee.

Ellen crossed her legs, tossed her hair back and placed her arms on the table. Her lips parted but she made no sound. She hadn't touched her scone.

Peter sat waiting in anticipation for her reaction; his gaze never left Ellen's face until she reached out, placed her hand on his and spoke.

"You'll find your mother, Peter, I just know it."

"It will have to wait I just finished my first year at Trinity."

"Trinity!" Ellen's eye brows shot upward.

"Yes, I enjoyed it, great teachers and interesting classes."

The following Friday evening as Peter, Connor and Hannah entered Donovan's, Ellen appeared before them. "Greetings." She tilted her head and focused her eyes on Peter.

"The bookstore. You're looking fine," said Peter. And she did. Her brown hair cascaded down her back and she looked directly at him with her brown eyes. She wore a yellow sweater draped around her shoulders with the right amount of cling to show off her curves and jeans which made her look most alluring.

There were four seats at the bar. Ellen steered Peter to the one on the right. She sat to his left which left the other two seats for Hannah and Connor.

"Getting ready to go back to Trinity?" Ellen asked.

"Yes, I leave in two days. How's business in the book store?"

"It's okay but it's boring work until someone comes in looking for books on adoption."

Ellen slipped an arm through Peter's and whispered. "Walk me home."

Hannah and Connor turned their heads to watch the couple leave.

It was a warm September evening, voices from pubs flowed out into the street; people sat on a wall overlooking a river enjoying the wash of good weather. Ellen's arm remained linked to Peter's.

"How are your books on adoption?"

"Good, at least I'm getting to understand how people go about it but not why a woman would give up her baby."

"Sometimes mothers give up their babies because they are too young. Maybe that's what happened to yours? Do you think your mother is still in America?"

"Maybe."

"I'd love to live there. Must be exciting."

"Would you?"

"Yes." *Anything to get out of here.*

Upon arrival at her house she turned to him and kissed him on the cheek which surprised Peter.

"Are you free tomorrow?" she asked standing very close and looking up at him.

"Yes, I have some time. Why?"

"Good, stop by the bookstore, I'd like to say goodbye to you before you leave for Dublin."

She laid a hand on his chest.

"I will."

The next morning Peter headed out to the bookstore and Ellen Adams. Ellen was busy with a customer when Peter walked in and he watched as she charmed a woman into buying two books, one on gardening and one on cooking. Once the woman left Ellen and Peter were alone. Ellen wrapped her arms around Peter's neck and kissed him on the lips. Her lips were moist and soft, Peter became aroused.

"That's your going away present, come see me when you come home from Trinity College."

He held her close and then kissed her again, this time deep and long. "That's so you'll remember me."

Peter arrived at the front gates of Trinity and saw a limo driving up. A classmate of his, William Duxbury, was getting out of the back seat. The driver got out and removed three suitcases from the trunk. William strode by Peter ignoring his presence.

It was customary for teachers to sit with students returning for the fall semester in the dining room for supper. William and Peter happened to sit at the same table. The teacher struck up a conversation with Peter asking him what he did over the summer.

"I worked on my grandfather's farm." William Duxbury rolled his eyes and jabbed the student sitting next to him who laughed. Peter noticed but ignored the gesture.

Classes began the next day. Peter sat in the third seat and William Duxbury sat behind him.

He leaned in and said. "Must be hard being adopted, not knowing who you are and having to shovel cow shit for the summer."

Peter turned and said. "Not at all, think about where your hamburger comes from."

"Mr. Shea, no talking in class," said the teacher.

When the teacher turned toward the black board William leaned in.

"Yeah, shut your mouth."

Peter seethed but kept quiet.

William Duxbury was the only son of the Duxbury family who owned hotel chains in Ireland and Massachusetts. His mother was his advocate but his father was his nemesis, always wanting more than William could produce and was not pleased when William finished in the bottom half of his class, a fact he reminded him of over the summer.

At any opportunity William Duxbury goaded Peter who held his temper trying to keep from confronting William even when he asked his friends within hearing distance of Peter, how a farmer's grandson could be first in their class.

One January morning Peter was walking across the campus against a strong wind and he felt a hand on his shoulder. He turned to come face to face with a scowling William Duxbury who shoved Peter almost causing him to fall.

"I don't want any trouble," Peter said as he righted himself.

"Yeh, well you're going to get it anyway," said William as he lifted his closed fist towards Peter's face.

Peter ducked and swung hitting William in the stomach who keeled over just as his teacher, Mr. Smith, rounded the corner.

"Mr. Shea. What are you doing?" he said as he helped William to his feet.

"He hit me," cried William.

"Follow me, both of you."

The boys stood in the teacher's office who demanded an explanation.

"He hit me," said William. "I didn't do anything."

"I apologize, it won't happen again."

Mr. Smith hesitated. "Mr. Shea. We do not tolerate that behavior at Trinity. I have no choice but to reprimand you."

"Yes, sir" Peter said.

"You are in excellent standing here, Mr. Shea." William grimaced. "You are not to attend class for a week. You may go to the library and dining hall only. You are excused, Mr. Duxbury but Mr. Shea, I would like to speak with you privately."

William left gloating.

"Now then is there anything else you wish to add."

"No, sir. Just that it won't happen again."

"Sometimes lessons in life come in strange ways and we can learn from them. You are to be commended for your performance here and I trust you will keep that up."

"Yes, sir. Thank you."

Peter left determined to stay as far away as possible from William Duxbury. It wasn't hard to do. William Duxbury moved to Boston over the summer with his family and once more Peter was safe.

For the summer Peter worked on his Grandfather's farm and his spare time was spent with Ellen whose charm wove a spell over Peter that reached into every crevice of his body. All Peter saw was an alluring, beautiful, charming woman who invaded his thoughts and kept him awake at night; he had to have her.

Most afternoons Peter stopped at the bookstore and chatted with Ellen until closing time, his eyes following her every move. Peter invited Ellen to his house to meet Donal and Hannah. Hannah prepared roast chicken, from the butcher that day, potatoes, carrots and cabbage fresh from their garden which was spread out on the table. Ellen turned the conversation to adoption.

"Peter told me about being adopted and maybe finding his birth mother. I think it's a fine idea."

"He has a home right here," Hannah said as she passed the carrots.

"Yes he does, but finding her would complete the circle."

"As I have said many times, first I'll finish Trinity then the search. Dinner is delicious, Hannah."

"Yes it is," said Ellen.

Ellen said goodbye after thanking Donal and Hannah. On the way home Ellen caught Peter's hand. He grasped it and she wrapped her other hand around Peter's arm. They took a short cut through the park and Peter stopped, turned to Ellen and kissed her passionately forcing his tongue into her mouth and holding onto her afraid if he let go she would disappear. They continued walking until they reached Ellen's place and said goodnight.

"I'll look for any other books on adoption that may interest you."

"Thanks. I'll call you when I'm home for Christmas."

Ellen walked in to her house and her mother was there waiting.

"Who's the new boy?" she asked.

"I'm going to marry him and move to America away from this boring place."

"You'll never make any man happy. Ever since you were jilted by Jimmy Walsh you have changed from being a loving person to a vengeful one."

"I'll show everyone in this town what I can do when I marry a tall handsome American and move to America"

"You'll never be happy. Leave that boy alone." Her mother shook her head and blessed herself.

"I most certainly will not."

Peter arrived home. Donal and Hannah were still up.

"She seems like a nice girl." Donal stated.

"I think I'm going to marry her, Dad."

Hannah couldn't believe what she heard and Donal only murmured "Hmm."

Chapter Twelve

❦

Over the Christmas holidays Peter asked Ellen to marry him which she accepted with a resounding "Yes!"

Peter returned to Trinity and devoted his time to his studies except for his weekly letter to Ellen, who wrote back immediately. Peter was still in awe of Trinity and the availability of classes, lectures, professors who appeared to like teaching. He met students from all over the world, listening to their command of English, observing their culture, and wiping out his memory of William Duxbury.

That spring Peter packed up and headed home, graduation was a year away.

The European Union allowed Irish farmers to sell their goods at a much higher rate than what was available to them in the only market open to them at that time, the UK, and with the presence of Robert and Delia and their children John O'Brien no longer needed Peter during the summer. His grandfather encouraged Peter to find work instead, knowing he was smart and educated.

A pharmaceutical company opened a plant in the next village. After reviewing Peter's application they hired him for their research and development department, at a salary he only dreamt of. Family name and money didn't matter; all that mattered was the ability to think, be creative and get along with co-workers. Peter had all that and more, he was loyal. He opened a bank account, purchased a car, bought Donal a meerschaum pipe, Hannah a string of pearls and Ellen a diamond ring.

Ellen, an interesting job and a handsome paycheck shifted Peter's goals and Trinity was losing its rank. No amount of reasoning from Donal or Peter's grandfather to finish could convince Peter to do so. His mind was made up he would withdraw from Trinity and marry the woman he loved.

Peter presented Ellen with the diamond and she showed it off to whoever was interested

Peter and Ellen were married in a small church in Ellen's village. Ellen looked radiant in an ankle length white dress with white sandals. A crown of daisies circled her head as she was escorted by her father down the aisle. Her mother kept a stoic demeanor throughout the whole day. Ellen held her father's arm as he led her up the aisle to Peter who pulled at his blue stripe tie, eyeing the crowd who had come to witness the occasion and shifting his weight from one foot to the other until he saw Ellen. Their eyes met and everything stood still for Peter. After the ceremony, the guests moved to Donovan's for the celebration where Ellen danced with every available male there.

Six months later while Peter was washing the dinner dishes, Ellen asked him about his birth mother. "Where do you think your mother lives in America?"

"All I know is that I was born in Boston so she might be around there somewhere. I'm going to write to Tom in Massachusetts to see if he can shed some light on it. He just may know something."

"Better start soon."

"What's the rush?"

"It's just that you keep talking about it but don't do anything."

Peter dried his hands and wrapped his arms around Ellen as he attempted to kiss her but she turned her head to one side and his lips landed on her cheek.

"Let's go to Donovan's," she said.

"Sure."

There was a crowd around the bar. Ellen maneuvered her way in, leaving Peter behind who became distracted by a hand on his shoulder. He turned and saw Connor.

"Hey, old buddy," Connor said. "How've you been?"

"Great. Good to see you," said Peter shaking his friend's hand.

Their times together had been sparse since Peter got married, partly because Ellen always had some plans for them whenever Connor and Hannah wanted to get together.

"Where's Ellen?" Connor asked.

Peter looked around. "She's here somewhere." That's when he noticed her at the bar laughing and joking with a couple of guys.

"There she is," he said jerking his thumb toward the bar.

Conner, his hand wrapped around a glass, said, "How's married life?"

"It's good. We've been busy. Me with my job and Ellen has been working long hours at the book store."

"I see. By the way have you done anything further with your search for your mother?"

"Not yet, but I'm going to write to Tom to see if he knows anything. Then I'll see. I can't just show up in Boston without some kind of a plan."

"I would like to go with you but since I joined the farm with my father things are really busy so I don't think I can go. I am going to your father's for supper Sunday night. Why don't you and Ellen come? Good time to have long chat."

"We will. We will."

Peter made his way to Ellen and company.

"This is my husband, fellas," she said matter of factly.

They moved back to make room for Peter.

"Let's go home, Ellen." Peter stated as he took her arm firmly.

When they arrived home Peter stated they were going to his father's for supper Sunday night.

"Sunday night__" she started to say.

"Yes, Ellen, Sunday night."

"Suppose I don't want to go?"

"We are going together."

"Your sister hates me."

"She does not. I don't know where you got that idea. We are never with them anymore. You always have something else to do. Not this time, we are going and we are going together."

On Sunday evening the conversation slowly turned to Peter's search for his mother. At once Ellen became animated. "This is exciting. Ever since I knew Peter he has wanted this and now he has a plan."

"At the moment there is no plan. I am going to write to Tom, that's all."

"Well, that's a plan," said Ellen.

Hannah blanched at this exchange. "They are only talking, Ellen, beside__"

"That's more than ever before and I for one agree with it," she said as she circled her arm around Peter's shoulder.

Three months later Ellen was pregnant. Peter was overjoyed and became very solicitous of her. Ellen delivered a baby boy on October 3rd, 1979. They called him Liam. Peter tucked pictures of him inside a letter to Richard.

Peter held his newborn son in his arms and he thought of his mother. *How did she feel giving me up? A tiny infant. Did she have a choice? Has she ever wondered what happened to me? I've got to find her or at least try, especially now that I have a son. Maybe he will look like her, his grandmother. And Liam should know about her.* These questions continued to gnaw at Peter until he finally wrote to Tom.

Donal and Peter were sitting in front of the fireplace. Liam was in Peter's lap.

"I can see him looking more like you every day although he has Ellen's eyes."

"Dad, I can look for similarities on Ellen's side for Liam but I can go no further than myself on my side. This baby has to know both sides; this is the only human being I know that I have a blood connection to and I must find my mother so he will know where he came from." He paused and began again. "Now that I have Liam I wonder how she could just give me away. How was that for her? Did someone force her into it?"

Donal listened. "From the little we were told, there were young girls during that time that were pregnant and not married. That may have been her situation."

Peter leaned forward in his chair turned to Donal and said, "Dad, I'm going to start the search for my mother. I've written to Tom and Richard."

"Are you sure you want to do this? She may not want to see you. And now with little Liam..."

"That's exactly it, Dad. Liam will know his ancestry from Ellen's side and I hope to find mine for him and me. Maybe she'll not want to see me." Peter rose and paced. "At least I have to find out. Maybe Tom can help and Richard has always offered his help even when we were kids."

"I don't want you to get hurt. What will she be like? Maybe she's not a nice person. What is her life like now? Will she accept you if you find her? I can't imagine life without you, son. I guess that's what I fear most."

At that moment, Hannah arrived. She stared at Donal and Peter, who was cuddling Liam.

"I just told Dad, I'll be starting the search for my mother. I've written to Tom."

Hannah stared at Peter with dismay.

"This is no surprise. You all know I wanted to do this. Connor is busy on the farm but Richard and Tom can help me."

Hannah approached Peter as he was putting Liam into the car getting ready to go.

"You're being disloyal to Dad after all he's done for you," she reminded him. "And what about Liam? He knows us now. You can't take him away from us."

"Hannah," Peter held up his hand. "Nobody's going anywhere and I'm not being disloyal to Dad. He understands. Why can't you?"

"He doesn't like this any better than I do."

"Well, he's never said that to me."

"It's Ellen! She's wanted this from the very first. She wants to move to America."

"She's glad I'm doing it if it's what I want."

"It's just that you and I are so close and ever since Mom died there's always been the three of us and now Liam. We lost Mom and now you might go away."

"Look, I don't know where this is going to lead but it's what I want. Okay? I may stay right here but Liam needs to know his grandmother." He placed an arm around Hannah.

Hannah nodded but it didn't make her feel any better. She remembered an expression her mother used to use when something just wasn't right. *I've got a bad feeling about this.*

And that's how Hannah felt.

Chapter Thirteen

❦

One afternoon Donal was at home pondering information regarding Peter's adoption. He got up, walked to his bedroom and opened the bottom drawer to his bureau where he kept his papers. He picked up a large brown envelope and held it in his hands and as he did thoughts of Julia and himself the day they adopted Peter sifted through his mind. *We were so happy with this baby and Julia would be proud to see him as a father.* Contained in the documents was the name of the agency and the signature of the social worker who witnessed the adoption along with the signatures of Donal and Julia; there was no information about Peter's birth mother but perhaps this was enough for Peter to begin his search. Donal and Julia had discussed this before her death and both agreed when the time was right they would show it to him. In the back of his mind he knew this would be useful for Peter in his quest to locate his birth mother but family life, as Donal knew it, would change that he was sure of. Wrapping his sweater around him he clutched the envelope and headed to the living room placing it on a table next to his chair.

The door opened and Hannah meandered in followed by John O'Neil whom she had been dating for three months.

"You look serious, Dad. Must be big, you have a scowl on your face," she said as she stepped in front of the turf fire to warm herself on this damp April day.

"I have information for Peter which may help him find his birth mother," he said.

"What information?"

"It's for Peter's ears first."

Hannah narrowed her eyes, glared at her father and said. "Dad, I hate all of this. All this searching and wondering. I'm trying to understand. He does have a mother somewhere but we belong together now. We have everything we need here. And Liam. He's two years old and such a joy. If Peter finds her, he could move, take Liam."

"Peter has always expressed an interest in finding his birth mother. We all know that. When they gave him Liam wrapped in a warm blanket, the nurse said. 'He has your nose.' Peter remembers that and no one can say that to Peter."

"Finding your kin is important," said John O'Neil.

"I know, I know, but I love my brother and little Liam and would miss them so."

"No one's going anywhere, Hannah."

"At least not yet." was her reply.

On Sunday, Peter, and his family arrived at Donal's.

"Com'on, Liam. Walk with Daddy up the hill. We've time before supper." Peter stared at his three year old son seeing his wife's bright eyes and hair the color of his. These inherited traits always intrigued him. Being adopted gave him pause, wondering who he took after and why he liked certain things.

Holding his son's hand, they walked up the hill. Liam broke away from Peter's grasp and ran ahead chasing two rabbits darting around the field.

"Wait up, Liam," Peter called.

Peter caught up and stared at his son.

"Daddy, you look sad when you stare at me sometimes."

"I just wonder who I look like."

"You look like you, Daddy."

"I know but I'd like to know my real mother."

"Why do you think she gave you away?"

"She wasn't able to take care of me."

"Was she sick?"

"I don't know."

"I'm glad you didn't give me away. I'd be scared."

"Let's go back. I'm sure supper is ready."

Hannah scooped Liam up in her arms as soon as he entered and nuzzled his cheek. Liam responded by giggling and throwing his head back.

"How's my big boy today? My, you're looking so special today with your new cap and big boy shoes."

Liam removed his cap, handed it to Hannah and stuck out a foot, showing off his shoes.

After a supper of ham and cabbage they gathered around the fireplace.

Donal decided to tell Peter in front of all of them because he knew, at some point, they might be involved with the search. Giving Hannah advanced warning would lessen the impact on her.

"Peter, I have some information for you about your adoption which may or may not help you to search for your mother."

Peter ran his hand through his hair. "You do? Since when? Why haven't you told me of this before? What is it? How did you get it? Even Tom didn't have much for me to go by. Only the name of the adoption agency and with the birth of Liam I put the search off. Now you tell me you have something I should have known about a long time ago."

"I was waiting for the right time that never seemed to come. Part of which was because I was afraid of what would happen. I've had it since you were born. I kept it from you because like Hannah I, too, was scared, scared of losing you but it's the right thing to do. It's your adoption papers." Donal handed an envelope to Peter.

Ellen sucked in her breath then her lips formed a faint smile. Hannah clenched her jaw.

"Inside you will find the name of the social worker who witnessed your adoption and the adoption agency. She might be still there. Your mother would have agreed. Find your birth mother with my blessing. Godspeed, son."

The only sound was Liam's chatter. Peter opened the envelope and scanned the pages, yellow from age, and then focused on the signatures. Donal's and Julia's were there along with the name of the witness, a social worker named Ann Marie Hale. Peter's hands trembled slightly, he felt light headed but he read on. Ellen looked over his shoulder. The silence was broken by a loud crash; Liam had knocked over a jar filled with marbles spilling them all over the floor.

"Do you think she might still be there after all this time? That was twenty five years ago."

"As I remember her she was quite young then, sort of new to adoption but most sincere and took a special interest in you as I recall her saying we were getting a special baby."

"Do you think she would have known my mother?"

"I don't know, maybe. You could go there and find out, stay with Tom, see Richard."

Hannah broke the silence that followed.

"John and I have something to tell you all."

John stood to his full height of six feet and pushed his black hair away from his forehead and before Hannah could say another word, John blurted out. "I've asked Hannah to marry me and she said yes."

The heavy aura that had blanketed the room changed to one of happiness and congratulations all around as everyone was on their feet wishing them well.

Peter's insomnia started with this new piece of information. He would wake from a dream about a tunnel with no way out. Often he would fall asleep in the chair with his adoption papers dangling from his hand.

"Peter, aren't you hungry?" asked Ellen.

"Not very." He answered moving his food around on his plate.

"Too much thinking and wondering if I'm doing the right thing. I always thought I wanted this and now..."

"Now what?"

"I'm not sure."

"Well be sure. This is what you always wanted. You can't turn back now. Maybe she wonders what happened to you. Did you ever think of that?"

"Yes, but what if she didn't?"

"Stop thinking that way. Write to Tom again."

It was late afternoon when Tom picked up his mail. He noticed the return address on a letter. It was from Ireland. He opened it and read Peter's request to find Ann Marie Hale. Seeing her name it all came back to Tom including her role in the adoption of Peter but he had forgotten who she was. He looked up the number of the adoption agency in the telephone book and dialed it recalling the loss they felt when Julia died. He had reservations about Peter's search but would put them aside to do whatever he could to help his nephew. Tom explained to the person on the other end of the phone that he was looking for a social worker who witnessed his nephew's adoption in 1957.

"All our records are confidential, sir."

"Would you at least tell me if a social worker by the name of Ann Marie Hale still works there?"

"Sorry, sir, I cannot do that. If you leave your number someone will get back to you."

After an interminable week, Tom received a call from Ann Marie Hale.

"Yes, I remember that couple. You are her brother, you say? What can I do for you?"

Tom told Ann Marie Peter's story and of his determination to find his birth mother.

"My sympathy on your loss. We cannot give out information that would breach the confidentiality of the birth mother's identity. Any request would have to come from the adoptee, not a relative. I can give out non-identifying information but only to the adoptee and he has to come here in person in order for me to give that out. Where does your nephew live now?"

"Ireland. My brother-in-law moved back there after his wife died."

"In order for me to give him any information I will need identification such as a passport or driver's license."

"Thank you very much." Tom hung up the phone and sent a quick note to Peter filling him in on everything that had transpired.

Peter read Tom's letter aloud to Ellen who was seated in a chair cradling their newborn daughter, Fiona. Neither one of them spoke. He had very little to go on but pieces were falling into place and each piece attached itself to a spool to form useful threads that could be linked together. This was the beginning of a long journey. Peter must take the next step himself but his emotional state of indecision kept him prisoner. Searching for an answer, Peter's finger stroked Fiona's cheek. His children had a grandmother somewhere. It was up to him.

"Now I have two reasons to find my birth mother."

"It's about time. Better get started," said Ellen.

"I'll settle things at work and leave as soon as I can. I'll stay with Tom, call Richard and pay a visit to Ann Marie Hale."

Chapter Fourteen

❧

Peter and Connor were in the den. Connor watched with dismay as Peter fumbled around looking for his passport and muttering to himself. It was almost midnight. They had been over this before. Peter's myriad of excuses to avoid travel was frustrating for Connor and was grating on Ellen.

"Look, Tom is waiting for you. What is the matter? You can't make plane reservations without a passport. Now find it and let me know when you do and we'll go to the travel agent together."

"What are you waiting for? All I heard was how much you wanted to find your mother and I see no evidence of that happening. You've got to make a start. Even Connor has given up on you." Ellen shouted over the cries of Fiona.

"This information opened a path for me that I cannot and will not ignore, but I must do it in my own good time not according to anyone else's. It was twenty six years ago, that's a lifetime and things may be different for her now. I have to think about rejection and interfering with her life. Does that make me want to discard the search? No, but I must be prepared for what could happen."

"I thought we would be on our way to America by now."

"Is that your reason for pushing me on? Is that all you care about?"

Ellen left the room with Fiona on her hip.

Since taking possession of his adoption papers Peter would startle at loud noises, he ate little and most nights Ellen would find him asleep in front of the television. Every night he sat at the edge of one of the children's bed until they fell asleep.

One morning Peter sat swirling the tea in his cup staring into space. Ellen walked in carrying Fiona followed by Liam in his pajamas. Before she could speak Peter announced. "I've called Connor. I have my passport. As soon as I can get my tickets I'm off to America. Connor will drive me to the airport."

Peter felt drained. Lack of sleep left dark circles under his eyes. His unkempt hair partly covered his forehead. His breath came in heavy sighs.

"You look like you could use a good breakfast. I'll fix you one and then get yourself cleaned up and get a haircut." Ellen commanded placing Fiona in Peter's arms.

Connor arrived the following morning, they drove to the travel agency and Peter left with a round trip ticket to Boston.

Peter watched rain pelting the window panes and saw wind whip through branches of a Maple tree trying to break them loose from their trunk. Peter rubbed his chin, stood and kissed Ellen and the children. "Daddy will be back soon," he told them. Connor drove him to Shannon Airport in Ireland for his flight to Logan Airport in Boston

Tom picked him up and they headed to Curran's for food and a pint where they were met by Richard, who was still taller than Peter. The friends shook hands and Peter filled him in on the latest information and the plan to meet Ann Marie Hale as he retrieved pictures of Liam and Fiona from his billfold.

"These are the reasons I need to at least locate her and see if she wants to see me and them."

"The town hall has information on births, deaths, marriages and so forth. Worth taking a look there providing Ann Marie

Hale gives you something to go. I am at your disposal and can drive you around to places."

"That would be a big help."

"Good," said Tom. "I had no intention of letting you lose, especially in my truck, so when Richard told me he would cart you around I gladly accepted. However I would like to go with you tomorrow as I want to meet Ann Marie Hale," said Tom.

"What time are we meeting her?" asked Peter.

"Your appointment is for ten o'clock."

Peter's stomach lurched

"What is it? You've been acting strange ever since you arrived. Are you alright?"

Peter wiped his lips with a napkin and stared at his food.

Ever since Peter found out about Ann Marie Hale and her connection to his adoption Peter's perspective of finding his mother had changed. He was overcome with doubt.

Will I be invading her privacy? Has she forgotten all about me? What would the next step be? Am I being fair to my father and Hannah? This is what I have wanted and yet all this uncertainty continues to torment me.

"I'm fine." Peter managed to say.

Tom placed a hand on Peter's arm. "We'll go to my place where you can get a good night's rest and we'll leave around nine."

A good night's rest, Peter thought, I don't know what that is anymore. I'm tired but I can't sleep. I'm hungry but I can't eat. This search occupies my mind day and night. It's taken hold of me and I can't shake it.

Tom drove into the driveway of his house once occupied by Donal, Julia, Peter and Hannah. Peter's memory of soft spoken Julia, her red hair, her warm embrace flooded his mind. He stood in the driveway remembering the day they left for Ireland. If his mother had lived would he feel the need to search for his birth mother? He would never know the answer.

The next morning Peter, Richard and Tom were ushered into Ann Marie's office. Peter produced his papers and when she was satisfied she gave Peter information regarding his mother. "She was white, seventeen, unmarried, no medical problems, high school student, middle class family".

Peter sat immobile. His mother was real. *She was young, in high school and unmarried. She must not have had a choice, especially back then. Maybe she would have kept me if she could.* This thought was encouraging but did not allay his fear of rejection.

"Let me know when you are ready to continue."

Peter's arms were limp, his body weighted down by information. At last he nodded.

"Some birth mothers may now have another life and do not want their child's existence known. Keep that in mind. Now in your case, your birth mother left you a letter." She opened the folder as she spoke.

Peter felt numb. "A letter, from her?"

"Yes, from your birth mother. I was instructed to put it with your papers by your mother." Ann Marie said as she handed him a cold glass of water which he finished in one swallow.

Wiping his hands on his legs he managed to say.

"So you knew my mother?" Peter asked.

"Yes, I did."

"What was she like?"

"She was sweet, full of love for you and sad to give you up but bear in mind she has another life now which may not include you although you may already know that. How was your adoptive family?" *I tried hard to match him up with the best I could find at that time.*

"My Uncle Tom here," Peter said pointing to Tom. "is my mother's brother and he and my parents cared a great deal for us and loved us. My mother died when I was thirteen and that's when I want to find my birth mother."

"Your uncle told me of your loss. I am sorry. I knew them as well."

Joy and anxiety caused Peter to feel irrational until he waited, waited for the demons to dissipate before he spoke.

"May I see the letter?"

Ann Marie handed it to him and said.

"You may want to bring the letter home and read it in private or you can open it now if you like. In any case it's yours. We don't often have this situation. Sometimes letters sit in the file. No one claims them. Sometimes there is nothing there for people who do come. I hope this helps in your search."

Peter looked down at the envelope; Baby Porter was written on the outside of it, the seal still intact. Richard and Tom sat there waiting.

"I'll take it home." He stood and thanked Ann Marie and headed out the door followed by Tom and Richard.

"If you need anything or if there is anything I can do for you, Peter, please call. Tom has my number. Good luck."

Peter clenched the letter in his hand never uttering a sound during the ride home. He walked in the front door, headed for the living room and slid into a chair.

"Tom, will you read it out loud?"

"Sure."

Peter opened the envelope and a tangled chain attached to a four leaf clover fell out. He held it in his hand and handed the letter to Tom.

Dear baby,

You didn't ask to be born but here you are and here am I. I am your mother and I am seventeen years old and unmarried. Girls like me are sent away to have their babies and are forced to give them up for adoption. My mother and father felt shamed and embarrassed by my pregnancy.

I had no choice but to give you up but my love for you will never go away. I won't let it go away. I hope the family that adopts you will love you and take care of you. The social worker told me adoptive parents love their children as their own. That made me feel a little better but I wish I was the one who was going to take care of you. I have enclosed a four leaf clover given to me by my best friend. It's yours.

Tom took a deep breath and exhaled slowly. Peter stared at the letter holding on to the words trying to control the eruption he felt in his chest.

Tom looked up. "Do you want me to go on?"

"Of course."

Tom cleared his throat.

I have asked that this letter be placed with your adoption file in case you should try to find me. I hope someday you will. I will think of you all the rest of my days.

Maggie Porter, Peabody Mass September 2, 1957

Peter cried openly, relief washed over him. His mother was real, she loved him and hated giving him up.

"Well, you've got name and a place," said Tom gently. "Do you want to continue your search? It may be a long road for you and you may need to spend some time here. Are you sure this is what you want?"

"Yes. I'll continue the search. Richard?"

"I'm in for the long haul. I'll be back in the morning, have the coffee ready. I'll bring doughnuts"

"Sounds good," said Peter.

"Peter, keep in mind, she wrote this after you were born. That was twenty seven years ago. She may feel differently now. Her life could have changed," said Tom.

Rubbing his forehead, Peter sat and read the hand-written letter over and over again. He held the four-leaf clover in his hand. Something of hers. When he was finished he carefully folded the yellowed letter and placed it back into the envelope along with the four-leaf clover. No matter what it took and no matter how long it would take, he would continue his search.

Chapter Fifteen

〜

The next morning Richard arrived with fresh doughnuts and joined Peter in the kitchen. His and Hannah's drawings, the smell of Julia's cooking and the presence of warmth were long gone. Instead, in its place was a pan in the sink with a wooden spoon stuck to it, a pizza box on the counter and a toaster-oven with a thin veil of dust on top of it.

"Okay, let's pour coffee and start with a jelly doughnut," said Richard. "We've got four days to explore before you have to leave but let me say this. Whatever we don't accomplish you can always come back or I could continue. Agree?"

"Yes," said Peter as he bit into a doughnut and slurped his coffee.

"First thing is the town hall. We have a name, so we will start there."

"But what if..."

"Never mind the what ifs. That has to be her father's name. Got to be a Porter somewhere."

"Also the place she lived. Peabody. Let's map this out. We drive to Peabody and see what that brings us."

"Now you're thinking. Finish up, let's go. You know this is just the beginning."

"In Ireland you can find birth certificates, death certificates, marriage certificates and can find someone who knew them or their families and can tell stories about each and every one of them."

"This isn't Ireland it's America where people move and change cities and jobs."

Richard drove to the town of Peabody and at his insistence pulled into a pizza place for some refreshment and a cold drink. Peter's hunger was for information not food.

The waitress wiped the counter from side to side eyeing the strangers before her.

"New in town or just visiting?" she asked moving the cloth closer to the edge where they were seated.

"Just visiting. Trying to find an old friend who used to live here."

"And who might that be?"

"Maggie Porter."

"Never heard of her. Would you like to order?"

The cook in the kitchen heard the entire conversation and spoke to the waitress when she walked in to place their order.

Thirty minutes later they were on the street heading toward their car with no further information. When they left, the waitress lifted the telephone receiver from the wall and dialed Maggie's number.

They reached the town hall at two o'clock. A sticker was posted on the front door. The town hall closed at noon on Wednesdays.

"Great, we've lost a day."

"Well maybe not. Let's stop at the library. They know everything that goes on."

They jumped back into the car and drove off.

"Supposed she is married, then what?"

"She's got to have a birth certificate."

"What if she wasn't born here?"

"Well she lived here at some point."

"Maybe she moved after she had me. I have the letter and her name. If she was seventeen when I was born she must be forty three now, born in 1940."

"Good, now you're thinking."

"Here's the library."

She may have grown up here. Maybe went to school here.

Richard went in, Peter waited in the car.

"Excuse me. I'm looking for directions to the Porter's house." said Richard.

"Are you a relative?" the woman at the desk asked?"

"No, but a friend of mine is. I'm actually looking for Maggie Porter."

A man checking out three books glanced at Richard. "I knew an Ethan Porter. Played basketball with him in high school. Seems he had a sister, older. She left in her junior year. Never did come back. I think their father is still living in the house. Their mother died a long time ago."

"Was the sister's name Maggie?"

"Yeah, come to think of it, it was."

"Do you know where they lived?"

"No I don't but a visit to the town hall will have that information."

"Thanks for the tip." Richard made a hasty exit headed for the car and jumped in next to Peter.

"Some guy in there knew the Porters, Ethan, and said he had a sister who left school early. Said go to the town hall for records. Our work for today is finished. Come on. Let's go."

In the morning they drove to the town hall and pulled into the parking lot. Peter was first out of the car and first to enter the town hall. He glanced at a board with names of departments and locations. Richard pointed to the City Clerk office. They climbed two flights of stairs and walked into the clerk's office.

"Can I help you?" asked a woman sitting behind a desk cluttered with papers and two telephones.

"Yes," said Peter. "I'm looking for a birth certificate."

"Two doors down on the right hand side. They have what you need."

I hope so.

Peter and Richard walked into a chaotic room. Phones ringing, people going from one desk to another, amiable chatter, typewriters clacking and amidst all this a young woman with a broad smile greeted them.

"What can I do for you? You both look serious must be looking for a dead rich uncle."

Peter's shoulders relaxed and Richard laughed aloud.

"I'm looking for a birth certificate of Maggie Porter born in 1940."

"I'll see what I come up with. Do you have a date?"

"No, just the year."

Fifteen minutes passed when finally the woman came back. No Maggie Porter.

Peter thought for a minute. "How about a death certificate for Porter."

"First name."

"I don't know."

"This is tough. Tell you what, I'll pull the files we have on the Porters and see if we can put the puzzle together."

A half an hour later the woman came back with several records.

"I found a Joan Porter's death certificate and a Mairead Porter's birth certificate and Ethan Porter's birth certificate all at the same address."

"You must have worked for the FBI," said Richard

"Mairead is Irish for Margaret and Maggie is a nickname for Margaret," said Peter.

"Can we have copies of those three?" asked Peter, his excitement mounting

"Coming right up. Glad to be of service."

Peter held on to the counter waiting for the copies, his mother's birth certificate, his grandmother's death certificate and his uncle's birth certificate.

Once back in the car. Peter read his mother's birth certificate and the address where she lived at the time.

"Want to drive by the house?" asked Richard.

"No. I want to go home, to Ireland, and talk to Ellen and my father. And I need to see my kids."

Peter's head was swimming with speculation, rejection and disappointment with what he would find. The closer he got the more fearful he became. Would the end result be more than he could handle? *Did her family disown her? Maybe they don't know where she is.*

The unraveling of his roots was overwhelming. He could go no further. Peter left for Ireland and did not return for three years. Richard wrote faithfully and Peter responded. Richard continued the search on his own and would be ready when Peter returned to America.

Chapter Sixteen

༄

Maggie's job at the school library ended for the day and her face lit up when Frances and Emma came through the front door with eager smiles on their faces as they rushed to their mother for hugs and kisses. The girls would chatter about school, their friends, their teachers and any other subject which came into their minds. Being the last one to finish at the school library Maggie locked up and the trio headed for their car in the school parking lot. She did not notice the car that had been there every day that week parked in the visitors section with a man sitting behind the wheel. He drove away after their car turned onto the main road.

She thought about the unsettling phone call she received from Helen. Two young men came in for pizza and asked if she knew Maggie Porter. Helen commented that one of them sounded as if he had an Irish brogue.

Impossible. How could there be a connection but still... She put it out of her mind for now.

Maggie turned the keys in the ignition. Today was his birthday, twenty-eight years old. He could be married with a family of his own and she could be a grandmother. *I hope he's happy.* She gripped the wheel of the car as she turned into the driveway.

"Mom, that was a quick turn. You must have been thinking of something else," exclaimed Frances.

"Yes, I was." She pulled into driveway and the girls got out rushing into the house.

Maggie leaned her forehead on the steering wheel. *I must talk to Joe tonight about telling the girls about my son. Frances was to enter college that fall. Will she be afraid? What if her friends find out? And Emma, dear sweet Emma. Will she stop coming into our bed at night to lie beside me until sleep overtakes her?*

Maggie had lived with the secret long enough. She needed to unlock the door and tell her daughters. She reached for her purse and her knitting bag and as she left the car a ball of yarn slipped out and rolled down the driveway leaving a single strand of yarn in its wake.

Maggie entered the house dropping her keys and her purse on the counter with a thud. She leaned on the kitchen sink bending her head looking for answers.

How will I tell them? What will I say?

"Drop something down the sink?" Joe asked as he walked into the kitchen.

"It's about my son. I want to tell the girls."

"What good will that do? What will they think or say? That part of your life is over, let it be, Maggie, let it be."

"It will never over for me, Joe, I told you that."

"I can't understand what good it will do. They'll never see him, none of us will."

"How can we be sure of that?"

"I suppose it's possible but how..."

"Joe, it's the secret that's killing me. Everyone knows, you, Ethan, Dad. The girls have to know."

"I see your mind is made up. I hope this is the end of it. When do you want to tell them?"

"Now."

Maggie splashed cold water on her face, dried it, took a deep breath and went to the bottom of the stairs.

"Girls," Maggie called. "Can you come downstairs?"

"What's up?" asked Frances.

"Sit down. I have something to tell you."

"Mom, are you alright? You've been acting weird lately."

"She is not weird," said Emma in defense of her mother.

Maggie took a deep breath and started "When I was your age, girls who became pregnant and were not married, were sent away to have their babies. You see, times were different then. There was a lot of embarrassment for the family."

She glanced at each of her daughters, so different from each other in personalities but with similar looks. Looking from one to the other she felt her heart straining within the confines of her chest and with a trembling voice she continued.

"I was one of those girls." Enormous relief settled over her at least for a moment. She sat back in her seat and waited.

Frances's jaw dropped and Emma's eye brows shot up.

"You had a baby? What happened to it?" asked Frances.

"I had to give it up for adoption."

"You had to give up your baby!" exclaimed Frances.

"Where did it go?" asked Emma.

"I don't know. That's the worse part. I don't know. I was told adoptive parents loved their babies as their own and I can only hope this is true. I went to a home for three months until he was born."

"Did you see it?" asked Frances.

"Yes, I did see him for a short while. Everything was done quickly."

"You don't know who took it?" cried Emma.

"No. I don't."

"Did Grandpa and Grandma make you do this?"

"Yes. It was very embarrassing for them. I was very angry at the time. But I have both of you and my love for you has replaced that anger."

The girls looked at each other.

"Dad, did you know about this?" asked Emma.

"Yes, I knew before we were married. Mom decided that you both should know about this."

"Mom, I can't imagine doing this. You must have been right where I am now, finishing sophomore year. You had to give up school, your friends. Did you go back to school?"

"Not the same one. After the baby was born I went home and then to a private school to finish."

"How old is he now?" asked Emma.

"Twenty six."

"Giving up your baby...Mom that's awful. Do you think maybe we could find him?"

"I don't know. Everything was so secret in those days; I wouldn't know where to begin. What if he has a family and doesn't want to see me? What if he hates me for giving him away?"

"But if you find him you could tell him it wasn't your fault."

"A brother somewhere. Do you still think about him, Mom?" asked Frances.

"Yes, I do."

"They don't make girls give up their babies now, do they?" asked Emma.

"The shame may still be there, but I guess it depends on the family."

"My friend Joyce has a cousin who is adopted."

"She does?" Maggie asked.

"Yes, but it's no big deal."

"He must wonder where you are, Mom. Do you think his family told him about you?"

"I don't think that kind information was passed on."

"Remember, Mom had no choice. Grandpa did what had to be done and Mom sees that now but at the time she was heartbroken," said Joe.

Maggie wrapped her hands around her neck. She recalled the cold weight in her chest she felt that day as she left Swan Point. Were there any more hurdles?

The next day Maggie worked late at the library and the girls took the school bus home. As she came out of the building and headed toward her car a man approached her, calling her name as he walked. She turned to come face to face with George Cooper. She stopped and tightened her grip on her books. Words were forming in her mind but she could not get them out of her mouth.

"Maggie. It's been a long time."

George was pale, with a wrinkled brow and lackluster eyes. He appeared thinner than she remembered and somehow not as handsome.

"Why George, George Cooper," she managed to say.

"How are you?"

"Fine, fine. What are you doing here? Do you live here?"

"Not for long. I knew you had moved back and one of my friends told me you worked at the school."

"Yes, I am the librarian."

"Are those your daughters I see you leave school with?"

Has he been watching us? How long has he been doing this? She looked to see how far away her car was. *Was anyone else around?*

"Yes, they are. What about you are you married?"

"No, divorced. One of those things. Maggie__"

"George, I have a life now, please__"

"I never forgot you."

Maggie bent her head and rubbed her fingers across her forehead. George looked over her head at the school building.

"What happened to the baby?"

Maggie started to cry. "He was adopted."

"It was a boy?"

Maggie nodded.

"He must be grown by now. I wanted to see you before I left."

"Where are you going?"

"California. Going to join a law firm in San Francisco. Need a change."

"I wish you well. Good luck."

Maggie glanced at her car.

"Goodbye, Maggie."

"Goodbye, George."

When Maggie pulled out of the parking lot George was still standing by his car, watching her pull away.

The driving time from the school to home was twenty minutes but to Maggie it seemed like a long journey. The encounter with George perturbed her. She sat when the traffic light turned green. She missed a turn into her neighborhood. *Will it ever be over completely?* That night she tossed and turned. *'He must be grown by now. I never forgot you.' I was the one that had to leave school. I was the one who watched as they took my baby away.*

Will she tell Joe or just bury it? No, she will tell him. No more secrets.

That night Maggie was reading. The lamp on her side of the bed was lit. Joe had come out of the bathroom and was getting under the covers. Maggie laid her book down and removed her glasses.

"Joe."

"What's up?"

"George Cooper was outside the library when I left today."

"So, he's still around?"

"Not for long, he's moving to California."

"Good. How was it seeing him again? It's been a long time."

"Very awkward. I couldn't believe that I once thought I loved him. He looked forlorn and I almost felt sorry for him."

Joe waited.

"Joe, I remember something else. I wrote a letter to the baby and a social worker put it in his file with my four leaf clover." Her hand went to her throat. "I forgot about it. I can't remember what I wrote but I know I did write one and I put my necklace in it. And the social worker, what was her name? Ann, Ann Marie."

"Look. Get some sleep. We've had enough trips down memory lane for one night."

Joe closed his eyes and Maggie laid her arm over his chest. She hoped for nights healing the bur that stuck to her by day.

Chapter Seventeen

❧

Winter's blanket was lifting slowly, spring was waiting patiently. Walking through the Irish countryside Peter lifted his boot and leaned to one side just missing the very first bloomers poking out of the partially frozen ground, tiny crocuses were pushing up towards the sun. Peter bent down and gently pushed decaying leaves off the tiny flower. The earth's crust was no match for the persistent crocuses. Peter admired this tenacious jewel heralding in spring; he stood for a moment wondering what was keeping him from returning to America. Liam and Fiona were two reasons. He hated leaving them and occasionally he helped his grandfather on the farm. Looking down at the crocuses which added a touch of brilliance to the dull countryside he made his decision.

Peter stirred the Irish stew he had put together earlier and began to mull over his decision to return to America. He turned the stew off, tossed the spoon in the sink, and headed outdoors for a short walk before dinner. The smell of turf permeated the air. April had been rainy and cold but the days in May were warm and the nights cool.

The family broke out in song as Fiona blew out five candles to the tune of "Happy Birthday." She was on Peter's lap licking icing from her fingers. Peter rubbed her soft arm and began. "I've never lost the thought of finding my birth mother as you all know..." Peter cleared his throat. "I've decided to resume the search. I've got a name and an address. I am going back to pick up where I left off. I've thought about this most days for three years and I'll have no peace until I know. I've grown used to the fact that maybe she won't see me but I'll take that chance. I'll write to Richard and Tom."

Hannah, newly married, raised her eyebrows, and frowned. She placed her plate with the cake on it on the table, wiped her mouth and asked, "I thought this was over?"

"No, it isn't, Hannah. I'm going back to continue where I left off and finish the search."

Ellen's eyes never left Peter's face.

"I'll be gone for one week. I'll stay with Tom."

Donal set his eyes on Liam who was eight, playing with his toy soldiers, always asking how things were made and how the sun came up. His eyes moved to five year old Fiona nestled in Peter's lap, who never went anywhere without her blanket which over time had become thread bare.

"Dad, I don't know what will happen but trust me I have to go."

"I understand. You need to set this thing straight no matter what happens. You've waited long enough"

What would all this mean to the family? Would it change the way they were now? Would Peter be changed after this? Would he get hurt or would he be welcomed by his mother and if so, what then?

The following week, Peter left Shannon for the long plane ride to Boston. Various scenarios regarding his mother kept him awake. "Hello, my name is Peter and I am your son." "Hello, my name is Peter and I may be your son." "I have no son. Who are you?" or "I was born thirty years ago and I may be your son." "I don't think so." Click.

The affirming piece of encouragement was the letter and even more so was the four leaf clover. Peter clung to them like moss on a retaining wall. They were the key that would unlock the secret. All he had to do was to find his mother and tell her what he had to connect them.

Tom picked him up at the airport. Peter was thinner than Tom remembered. They drove back to Tom's place and started to outline their strategy. Peter called Richard who had done his homework.

"I'll be over in the morning. I've got a name, address and telephone number that is very interesting," said Richard.

The next morning Richard arrives and over coffee and eggs they planned to go to Peabody first and drive by the house.

The neighborhood was mature with overgrown shrubs and tall trees. The houses were set back from the street, driveways rose from the sidewalks to the garages and a path led to the front door. Numbered mailboxes stood at the end of the driveways. Most house were ranch style some were Cape Cod style. There were no visible signs of small children. Richard drove around allowing Peter to take in the sight of what might be the neighborhood where his mother grew up. Peter watched for the house number and found it, number two six five and he asked Richard to drive around again.

"Well buddy, this must be the place."

"I suggest we go home and talk about making a call to the occupant of that house, Henry Porter."

"Good idea," said Peter.

Richard spent the night and several scenarios were discussed involving the phone call until they agreed that Peter would be the one to call on pretext of an Irish genealogy project.

The following morning he dialed the telephone number which Richard had given to him. A man with a gruff voice answered.

"Yes."

"Hello. My name is Peter Shea and I am doing a genealogy project about the Irish. I would like to ask you a few questions."

"What kind of questions? How do you know I'm Irish?"

"Well, I did find your mother's maiden name and connected it to Porter whom she married."

This was a total fabrication and Richard was dumfounded.

"Well, what do you want, be quick, I haven't got all day."

"Do you have a family?"

"Yes, I live alone and my wife is dead. Anything else?"

"Was your mother born in Ireland?"

"Yes. Anything else?"

"Do you have any children?"

"Yes, one son, one daughter."

"I have you listed as Henry Porter. Is that right?"

"Yes. I've had enough of this."

"Just one more question. The names of your children."

"Mairead and Ethan." And he slammed the phone down.

Peter hung up and said, "I just talked to my grandfather, he has two kids, Mairead and Ethan. There's the Mairead again. That's gotta be her. He's her father. My grandfather." He shouted. "My first blood relative. Someone I'm related to. Wonder what he looks like."

Richard then gave Peter Ethan's telephone number.

"We'll call your uncle next and then we'll see."

A deep male voice answered.

"Hello."

"My name is Peter Shea. I'm from Ireland and doing a genealogy project."

"My grandmother was Irish."

"Yes I found that out during my search."

"She used to baby sit for me and my sister, Maggie."

Peter gave the high sign to Richard.

"Your parents were born here."

"Yes."

"Actually we are interviewing females for this project, so I wonder if you would give me your sister's telephone number."

"Sure. She moved back after our mother got sick. She's married now. So you're from Ireland?"

"Yes." Connor answered. "What is your sister's married name?"

"Maggie Carlson. She lives here in town with her husband and two daughters."

Peter fumbled with the telephone but with Richard's help he recovered.

"I would like to contact her. Do you have her number?"

Peter had all he needed, the search was over or had it just begun?

With his mother just a phone call away, reluctance again set in. Richard let his friend digest this last and final clue. Would this call upset her life? Would her family not want her to see him? Worse would she not want to see him?

Peter packed the information in his bag and said goodbye to Richard who said. "You've got all you need. It has been years and now you have the key to unlock your past. This is the hardest step because it will be final; there is no more information and you will have your answer. I understand your dilemma but you must make the call to be done with this once and for all."

"I'm going back home. I'll make the call from there."

Upon Peter's return to Ireland he slept little often falling asleep in front of the television. He returned to the fields where he walked and thought. One day after a particularly long walk he returned to his house where Ellen sat immersed in *House and Garden* magazine and he told her of his next and final step.

Her only comment, as she stood tossing the magazine on the floor was, "It's about time."

PART THREE

Chapter Eighteen

Peter sat at the kitchen table. It was five o'clock in the morning; the sun had yet to rise and the only sound was the dripping of the coffee pot. He ran his thumb over the paper on which was written his mother's telephone number. He rubbed his unshaven face and rose to pour himself a cup of coffee. Early morning progressed to mid-morning before he reached for the telephone and dialed the number. Hope found its way into his thoughts; after all it was his thirtieth birthday.

The packages were strewn on the kitchen counter. Maggie's purse hung from her shoulder. She held her keys in one hand and clutched the telephone in the other hand not believing what she had just been asked. "Did September 2, 1957 mean anything to her?" Her hearing became dulled, words formed on her lips but no sound came out. She managed to sit down, take deep breaths to calm her racing heart until she heard the voice on the other end.

"Are you alright?"

"Yes. Why are you asking me about that date?"

"I was born on that date."

"But what does that have to do with me?"

"I think you may be my mother."

This must be a hoax

"Who are you? How did find me?"

"My name is Peter Shea. My search to find you was difficult and tedious but each piece of information led me to another until it all fit."

It's not possible.

"I have a letter written by Maggie Porter dated September 2, 1957 and a four-leaf clover on a chain__"

"Where did get that?"

"From Ann Marie Hale."

Maggie was being assaulted by facts which only one person other than her would know. She looked around for help, her throat constricted, her temples throbbed, the telephone trembled in her hand. She waited until she could form words with her mouth.

"Are you alright?"

"Yes."

It all came back. The pain of loss and sadness which seeped into her bones when she signed the adoption papers giving up her son.

"This must be totally unexpected for you. It required enormous courage on my part to call and I hope you will forgive the intrusion but I had to find out if you were my mother. My adoptive mother died when I was thirteen years old and the urge to find you became lodged in my mind, I couldn't shake it. I went to college, got married and when my son was born..."

He has a son.

"...finding you became an obsession with me. I have an uncle in Boston who was with my parents when they adopted me and he remembered the name of the adoption agency and the name of the social worker, Ann Marie Hale."

There was a ring of familiarity in his voice. Was it George Cooper's? What does he want? Is he angry at me for giving him up?

If it turns out he is not my son, what then. But the letter, the four-leaf clover and Ann Marie.

"Where do you live?"

"Ireland."

"Ireland?"

"Yes. My father moved my sister and me there when our mother died. To be near family. They were both born there."

Family. He has a family. And his mother died. He grew up without a mother and here I was all the time.

"I'm sorry about your mother."

"Yes, it was hard. She was a great mother but my father pulled us through. After that I always hoped I would find you. My father was reluctant at first but he's okay with it now."

"Are you alright? I mean you're healthy and happy?"

"Yes."

"Just the fact you are alive and well and have a good life is more than enough for me."

"And you?"

"Married with two daughters."

"Our last child was a girl. Do they know about me?"

"Yes. My husband, Joe, knew before we were married. No secrets. And we decided it would be best if the girls knew just in case you showed up."

"Did you think I might?"

"No. I always hoped I would see you again but I didn't give it much chance. You must have been very persistent."

"Yes, I was. Do you think we might meet each other?"

"I need to think this through and I must talk to my husband."

"Of course. It was good hearing your voice, for the first time, hope I hear it again," said Peter.

"You will. Give me your address and phone number. You'll hear from me after I talk to my husband." Maggie wrote it down and said goodbye

Maggie walked into the living room and slid into a chair clutching Peter's address. She covered her face with her hands and sobbed. The astonishing and totally unexpected phone call left her frantic. Her past came crashing down on her and the strength of it impacted her once more.

I must tell Joe. How will he feel? Will he want to see him? Maybe he doesn't want any part of him? And the girls, what will they say to their friends? Will they be embarrassed? All along I thought I wanted this and now I just don't know.

The hard work was just beginning but at last she knew he was safe, happy and loved.

Chapter Nineteen

❧

In the week that followed Peter's phone call, Maggie misplaced her car keys twice, missed a dental appointment and broke Joe's favorite coffee cup. Driving the car, she tried to picture what he looked like and tried to capture the sound of his voice when she slammed on the brakes, just missing a squirrel. She imagined him arriving on her front porch. What would she say? Would she recognize him?

This isn't happening. It must be a cruel joke. I did leave a letter and the four-leaf clover with the chain. The only one who would know this would be my son. Still, there is doubt. After all this time I will not have my life and my family's life turned upside down. What if I say no and he shows up and with a wife and two kids. Then what?

Her situation became intolerable, her tasks became daunting, and sleep became impossible.

Two weeks had elapsed since the phone call from Peter. Emma and Frances were watching television and Joe was mowing the grass. Maggie was browning chicken, sautéing vegetables and dicing the ingredients for a salad.

"Mom, where are my gym shorts? You said they were in your car and they are not there," said Emma.

"I cannot keep track of your stuff!" She slammed the utensil down on the stove top and flew out the back door. The smell of burning food brought Joe to the kitchen. He passed Maggie on the top step of the deck, her chin in her hands, her elbows resting on her bent knees. He continued through the back door, turned off the stove, and joined Maggie.

"What is going on? You have been off somewhere else for the past two weeks."

"Dinner is burned, let's get Chinese take-out." she said. They arrived at the restaurant and ordered a glass of wine while waiting for their order.

What if he does come for a visit? How will that change my life? Will he have any resemblances to either of his sisters--his half-sisters? Suppose he wants to see me because he's angry I gave him up.

"What is it? What's wrong with you?"

"Joe, he called."

"Who?"

Maggie hesitated.

Joe took a deep breath. "How did he find you?"

"Remember the letter I told you about? He got the name of the adoption agency from his father. He has an uncle in Boston that was there when he was adopted and he followed through with every lead until he found me. He has the letter I wrote and the four-leaf clover necklace that I left with it. It has to be him, Joe. He sounds fine. He's married with two kids, has a sister and lives in Ireland."

"Ireland! And he has two kids!" Joe shook his head. "How did you leave it?"

"I told him I would talk to you first. He gave me his address and phone number. What should we do?"

"What does he want? Why after all this time does he want to see you? I don't get it."

"Joe, he thinks I am his mother and I want to find out if it's true."

"You're not serious. What if he's unstable or something? We have Emma and Frances to think about. If he was close by we could meet him or something but Ireland! Where would he stay?"

"Joe, I have to do this."

"Let's sleep on it for a few days. Come on, our order is ready."

'I think you are my mother.' How can I be sure? All the indications are there. The letter, the four-leaf clover, his birth certificate. No one else would have that information or kept up the search.

In the days that followed she tried unsuccessfully to put Peter out of her mind. Would he be tall, have her coloring, and a big smile?

How is her life going to change? Why should it change at all? And the girls. Maybe they don't want to see him. She abandoned him once. She would not do that again. She would see him.

One night when Maggie and Joe were in bed, Joe removed his glasses, put his book down, and turned toward Maggie who was staring straight ahead.

"I need to see him, Joe."

"If you want him to come for a visit it's fine with me. Ask him to come by himself. It will be less overwhelming for us and only for a short time, like three nights. We need to tell the girls, the sooner the better."

They agreed to tell them the next morning.

Maggie was in the kitchen by six o'clock putting out cereal bowls, blueberry muffins and making coffee. It was Saturday; the girls would be up by nine which gave her time to rehearse what she would say.

My son, suppose he isn't. Your brother, half-brother, suppose he isn't.

She retrieved a brownie mix from the cupboard turned on the oven and went about greasing the pan and stirring up the mix. She loaded the dishwasher with last night's dishes and put a load of laundry in the machine. She walked outside and replenished the bird feeder. When she returned to the kitchen Joe was drinking coffee and reading the newspaper. She joined him.

Emma came down first, then Frances both still in pajamas. When they sat down Maggie started her rehearsed lines.

"Remember when I told you I had a baby a long time ago that I gave up for adoption?"

They looked up from their bowls. Frances laid her spoon in her bowl, Emma licked hers. They nodded and listened.

"He called me and he would like to visit."

She waited for a response.

"Here, with us?" asked Frances.

"Yes."

"How did he find you?" asked Emma.

"It's a long story, it took him years."

Maggie repeated what Peter told her.

"We have a brother, a sister-in-law and a nephew and a niece. I think it's awesome," said Emma.

"Our family has doubled in size. How old are his kids?" asked Frances.

"I think he said eight and five. They live in Ireland. I am inviting him to come for a visit."

"Ireland!" said Frances.

"Yes. We are going to invite him for three nights. He'll stay with us."

"Just him. After all we don't know him. We do have a life now," said Joe.

"He only wants to meet Mom," said Emma.

"It took him all these years. I think he's looking for more," said Joe

"It's just a visit. If it were me I'd want to see my mother," said Frances.

"I want to meet him. I must see him," said Maggie. At that moment Maggie walked away from her past and stepped into the future.

Maggie set her coffee cup on the table, wrapped her fingers around it and let out a sigh. She would see a grown man not a baby. They were total strangers. He had grown up influenced by people she did not know. What perception did he have of her? Would he be angry at her for giving him up? She stirred the coffee, watching the swirl, remembering the sadness she felt giving him up. She removed the spoon, drained the coffee, and wrote Peter a letter inviting him for a visit. Six weeks later Peter was on a flight to Boston to meet Maggie.

On the ride to the airport to pick Peter up, Maggie consulted her mirror several times.

"Any change?" asked Joe.

She dropped the mirror in her purse and snapped it closed. In the waiting area of the airport Maggie paced, Joe read the newspaper and Emma and Frances took in all the sights until Peter's flight landed.

Am I ready for this? I can't sit still. Suppose I don't recognize him. He won't know who I am. How will I know him?

Maggie looked toward the door where passengers would disembark and spotted Peter immediately when he walked out. He looked exactly like George Cooper, the square chin, tall, with dark brown hair. It was at that moment she knew he was her son.

"Peter, Peter," she called and waved. All her fears abandoned, she ran toward him, arms outstretched. He spotted her coming towards him, dropped his bag, and greeted her with open arms. She embraced the son she last saw thirty years ago. He was a grown man but the surge of love she felt when she saw him as a newborn repeated itself. Trembling she held him then released him to have a good look. After the inspection, she reached up to brush his hair away from his forehead.

Peter bent down and kissed her cheek, his tears mingling with hers.

They heard the hum of voices and people slipped by them unnoticed. Joe, Emma and Frances approached.

"Hello, I'm Joe and this is Emma and Frances."

Peter greeted his sisters with a warm hug.

"You're gorgeous lasses." They grinned from ear to ear.

Joe held out his hand and Peter responded with his.

"Welcome."

Joe grilled steaks and the girls made salad and baked potatoes in the oven. Maggie and Peter sat in the living room. Maggie noticed Peter's large hands like George Cooper's and his thin but wide grin.

"Tell me about your childhood."

"It was fine except when my mother died. My father took good care of my sister and me and my mother's family in Ireland were caring people. I had a good education and went to Trinity in Dublin for three years."

"Trinity! Three years. What happened?"

"Left when I was offered an interesting job with good pay and I was in love."

"Maybe you can finish someday. How relieved I am that you were happy and loved and had a good family."

"Yes, I was lucky."

"Maybe Ann Marie Hale had something to do with it."

The next morning Maggie drove Peter by her old high school. The guilt and sadness associated with her last few months there had vanished. Peter listened as she revealed the story of her pregnancy, her young life and how meeting Joe was a gift. He remembered the pizza place and the library and chuckled as he told Maggie he had already visited these places.

"We're both lucky Peter. Tomorrow we'll visit my father. I want you to meet him."

"He wasn't friendly on the phone when I spoke to him."

Because Maggie had missed all Peter's growing into manhood she couldn't get used to the fact that he was her son, it was the look and gestures of George Cooper inherent in Peter that convinced her it was so. He also possessed a grace in his mannerisms much like her mother.

"He'll be fine."

Peter grinned and again Maggie thought of George Cooper.

"You look just like your father."

"I look like someone. I've been waiting to hear that all my life.

"I told you not to let him come here," said Maggie's father on the telephone.

"Dad, he's my son. I couldn't do that."

"But you have a life now. That's all in the past."

"He is part of my past and yours. You did things because you thought it best. Now I'm doing something I think is best."

"I don't have to be part of this do I?"

"Yes. You're part of the family, as is Peter."

"It's too much for me. If your mother was here__"

"Mom would be delighted to see him."

"I don't know."

"It will be alright. Peter understands why I had to give him up."

"I suppose he blames me."

"There's no blame, Dad, only forgiveness."

"Have you forgiven me?"

"I have the girls now and I know I would do what I think is best for them and yes I forgive you. I did a long time ago. The past can drag us down if we let it. Peter and I will come over tomorrow for a visit, just him and I."

Henry rubbed his day old beard. "Okay, Mairead."

The following day Maggie pulled into her father's driveway with Peter in the passenger seat.

"This is where I grew up."

"Is this the house you lived in when you became pregnant with me?"

"Yes. I have happy and sad memories of this place and now they are part of a collection of my past which I cannot forget but I have a life now with Joe and the girls and it's more than enough for me."

Maggie got out of the car.

"Dad is expecting us. Come on, we'll go in through the side door."

Peter followed Maggie up the steps into the house. They walked through the kitchen into the living room. Henry was seated in his chair and slowly rose when Maggie and Peter came in.

"Hi Dad. This is Peter, Peter Shea, your grandson."

Henry swayed for a moment but recovered when Peter grasped his hand and shook it.

"Pleased to meet you, sir."

"Likewise. Sit down."

"Nice place you have here," said Peter.

"Thanks. The neighborhood has changed and of course the house isn't the same without my wife even though she's been gone a long time. Mairead tells me you live in Ireland."

"Yes, my father moved us there after our mother died."

"Lot of problems there in the north. Don't hear too much about it now. Were you involved in any of it?"

"No. Three of my uncles were and they were killed. I had to help my grandfather on the farm and I had my own family to think of. Peace talks have started both sides are resistant and it will take a while; at least most of the killing has stopped."

"Your grandparents lost four of their children. Hard for me to imagine."

"Yes it was tough on them but they have an enormous capacity for acceptance and strong family support."

"Would you care for a drink?"

"Yes, a beer would be fine."

"Maggie?"

"I'll have a glass of wine. I'll help you, Dad."

Henry got up and walked into the kitchen. Maggie followed him.

"Dad, are you alright?"

Henry turned his back to Maggie.

"You can turn away all you like but it won't change the fact that he is my son and your grandson."

"I know that now. He looks just like that Cooper fellow. I detested him for what he did to you."

"I realize that but none of this was Peter's doing. He's our flesh and blood. I am so grateful that he was well cared for and you should be too considering we gave him to strangers. Give him a chance, get to know him. He's family." Maggie's arm circled her father's shoulder.

"It all worked out," said her father.

"Because he had parents who loved him. Come on; get to know your grandson."

Henry looked at Maggie. The frown on his face softened, his lips parted.

"Please, Dad. Peter has two children which makes you a great grandfather."

Henry and Maggie walked back into the living room. Henry sat down, took a long swallow of his martini and set his glass down softly.

"Well young man, tell me about Ireland. I've never been there."

The evening before Peter was to leave Maggie invited Tom, Richard, Ethan and her father to join the family for dinner. Richard and Peter shared experiences of growing up together and finding Maggie. Tom participated in the conversation with thoughts of Julia and Donal while the family ate roast beef, mashed potatoes, fresh carrots and string beans.

The conversation turned to Trinity and Peter's decision to leave.

"You left at the end of your junior year," said Ethan.

"Yes, I wanted to get married."

"Must be a special lady."

"Yes, she is."

Emma and Frances thought it was romantic. Joe kept his opinion to himself as he cleared the plates to get ready for pie.

The following day Maggie drove Peter to the airport. Saying goodbye was sad yet joyous. They met, shared thoughts and now were going about the rest of their lives but it was not the last time they would see each other and they both knew it.

Chapter Twenty

∽

Liam and Fiona were asleep. Ellen and Peter were sitting in their living room discussing his trip to America.

"How did you get along?" asked Ellen.

"Fine, like we were never apart. It just felt right and I know she felt the same. I met her family. My sisters want to know what Liam and Fiona will call them," he laughed. "I have a family, just like you. Maggie says I look like my father but that was all she would say about him. They lost touch when she became pregnant," Peter said, as he sat in the chair, legs outstretched, hands clasped together around the back of his head. He closed his eyes. "Let's ask her to visit us."

"A visit, you say. Here with us?"

"That's right, a visit with her whole family."

"Well, I guess that would be a start. A start to get to know each other. Know what I mean."

"We missed all these years together and we've got to make up for lost time. We'll tell Dad and Hannah and I'll write to her to make arrangements. She's looking forward to meeting my father and, of course, you and the kids."

Ellen went into a frenzy of planning for the visit. She shopped for food they might like, cleaned the house from top to bottom. Hung new curtains in the guest room and purchased a new quilt, after which everyone was forbidden to enter. She purchased new clothes for herself and the children and told them they must be on their best behavior when the company comes from America.

We will need them when we move to America.

Noticing all the excitement, Peter asked Ellen if she was preparing for a state visit.

"Not at all. It's your mother's..." she stopped. "Your mother," she repeated. "I've not been able to say that since we've known each other and now I can."

"Now maybe you can understand how I feel. She never forgot me and always hoped I would find her. Are you glad they are coming?"

"Yes," said Ellen and turned her attention to washing the windows.

The Carlsons were due in at seven o'clock the next morning. Maggie and the girls stretched their necks looking out at Ireland, a land of green. The passenger door to the plane opened and the Carlsons were the first off. Peter approached them and embraced Maggie first, and then acknowledged Joe, Emma and Frances. "Welcome to Ireland," he said.

Peter pulled the car around to pick up his visitors. It was odd to see him sitting on the right hand side of the front seat of the car. Maggie and the girls managed to squeeze into the back seat and Joe sat next to Peter.

"My house is not far, we'll take the motorway and after the second roundabout we'll take a side road where you'll see the Irish countryside."

The side road was narrow and uneven and cars had to pull alongside a hedgerow to allow a car coming from the other direction to pass. They came upon open fields where the occasional thatched cottage and castle could be seen but it was the views forming a patchwork of all shades of green; heather waving in the soft winds against a backdrop of majestic mountains that was breathtaking.

"I've never seen such lush green. It's exquisite," said Maggie.

"It's our rainfall that makes it possible."

Traffic became dead slow and soon the reasons became known. On the right hand side of the road the backsides of several cows could be seen and they were in no hurry.

"There's no rushing them, we just have to wait," said Peter.

"Can we get out of the car?" asked Frances.

"Of course, this is Ireland where animals are people friendly."

Emma and Frances jumped out of the back seat and headed up to the cows for photos.

Further down the road they shared space with black faced sheep with markings on them and more cows coming in the opposite direction that approached the car, gave a casual glance at the occupants and plodded along. The family was delighted.

As they pulled into the driveway of Peter's detached, brick, bungalow, a wet rain started to fall. Stone walls defined the area between each of the houses.

Liam and Fiona ran out of the house before Ellen could catch them.

"Daddy," they screamed. Peter got out of the car, stooped and gathered them up in his arms. "I've not been gone long. Now let's go inside before you get soaked and I'll introduce you to some people."

Maggie was touched seeing Peter interact with his children. "This is my family from America," he said to Liam and Fiona. Liam stared at them and Fiona giggled.

"Dad, this is Maggie, my mother."

Donal approached with an outstretched hand.

"Pleased to meet you. Welcome to Ireland."

"Thank you. It's my pleasure and thank you for raising my son."

"He's a fine young man. I'm proud of him. This is his wife Ellen, his sister Hannah and her husband, John O' Neil."

They sat down in the small living room warmed by a fire while Hannah and Ellen served tea. Maggie noticed pictures on the mantle of Peter, Ellen, Liam and Fiona and one of a beautiful woman holding a chubby baby with a toothless smile.

"That's Julia and Peter," said Donal.

"She was beautiful and look at Peter as a baby," said Maggie. *I held him first.*

John O'Neil watched over the full Irish breakfast that Ellen had prepared for their guests.

Maggie turned to Ellen and said, "I missed out on Peter's life and I won't miss anymore."

"Neither will Peter."*I will see to it.*

Ellen and Maggie stood together in silence each with their own thoughts before sitting down at the table.

The rain ceased and Hannah pointed a rainbow out to Frances and Emma.

After breakfast, Peter and Maggie took a stroll into the village.

"How long have you been married?"

"Well let's see this is 1988 and we married in 1977 so it's eleven years."

"Your children are lovely. I can't believe I'm a grandmother. Hannah seems like a second mother to them."

"Yes, she is but one day she will have her own family."

"Peter," Maggie stopped and looked at her son. "I am so sorry about giving you up. I was seventeen, unmarried and forced into it. My parents thought it was the best thing especially for those days. But at least now I know you had good parents and a charming sister. And you have a family of your own. Some days the not knowing was unbearable. It eased after Joe and I had our girls but the wondering would ambush me when I least expected it."

"I had to know if you were still alive. After talking to your father I thought my search for you had ended and now look at us. The bond between a mother and child is unbreakable even in separation or death." Peter looked at Maggie. "No more of that. Ellen and I have talked about moving to America."

Maggie looked at Peter.

"You must be sure this is what you want. Most of your life has been here. Living in America will be different. All I want is what is best for you and your family"

"I spent thirteen years living in America so it is not altogether foreign to me and I still keep in touch with my friend who lives there and there's Tom. What's best for us is to live near you. My children have a grandmother now and that's what I want them to grow up with."

They turned to walk back and Maggie slipped her arm through Peter's and they continued on in silence.

Peter's memory of living in America was distant but memorable mostly because of his adoptive mother. He remembered her soothing voice and words of encouragement. How her red hair fell across her face when she read to him and Hannah. Peter remembered giving her daisies he picked from their yard which she placed in a jar and kept on the window sill under the kitchen window until there was nothing left but a stem. Now they were moving back and Peter refused to entertain any doubt of what they were about to do.

Peter took the group on a tour of the village. They stopped at the school he'd attended, where Maggie reflected on what his growing up years, of which she had no part, were like. Her sense of loss returned for a moment but was quickly dispelled when she looked at Peter who was standing in front of a swing set pushing Fiona. She looked over the valley and peace seeped in.

Joe, Maggie, and Peter were sitting outside waiting for supper, their last before going back to America.

"Ellen and I have talked it over and we want to tell everyone that our plans are to move to America as soon as we can. The sooner we tell them the better. They have an idea but hearing it may be difficult at first."

"Peter," Joe said, "just be sure this is what you want. It's a big step. Just be sure it's right for you and your family. What about Ellen?"

"Ellen is no problem. She's the one who suggested it. She's always encouraged me to find my mother. And she's more than happy to move to America."

"She is?"

"Yes. She thinks there is more opportunity there."

For whom?

"But you have a good job here," said Maggie.

"They said they may be able to use me in Boston."

"Well if that is what you want, I think it's a fine idea and you can stay with us until you get settled," said Maggie.

Joe folded his arms and frowned.

After their places had been cleared, Peter cleared his throat. Connor leaned into the back of his chair, Ellen's eyes were fixed on the floor, Donal searched Peter's face, Hannah, with her hands clasped together, sat next to John.

"Ellen and I are going to move to America. I want to be with my mother."

Connor remained silent while Donal stared at his son in surprise.

Peter reached across the table to Hannah. "I know this is difficult for you, Hannah. Please try to understand how I feel."

"Are you sure? Has anyone talked you into this?" She glared from Maggie to Ellen.

"Yes, I am dead sure. And no one has talked me into it."

Donal got up and walked to the window with his back to them staring out into Peter's back yard.

"Peter," Hannah said. "Why can't you just visit and they can visit us here. We're all that Liam and Fiona know. Please think about it."

"I have. We'll come back for a visit and you can visit us in America. You must remember how it was with our mother when we lived there?"

"But our life is here now and Liam and Fiona__"

"It's your life but not mine entirely."

Donal turned and looked at Peter, "Your mother and I taught you to think for yourself. We loved you as our own. I understand your need for kin. It's in our blood. America is not far away. Godspeed, Peter, and you, Ellen."

There was silence. Even Liam and Fiona knew something had just happened. They were staring at their grandfather.

"Are we moving to America?" asked Liam.

"Yes, we are."

"Will we take a plane?"

"Yes. We will."

"I get a window seat."

"You can both get a window seat," said Peter.

Connor stood up, raised his glass and said loud and clear. "To Donal for being a good father, to Hannah for loving Peter, to Peter for being a loyal friend, to Ellen for being a supportive wife and to Maggie for being an amazing woman."

"Slainte."

They raised their glasses all except Joe who wrapped his fingers around his.

"Promise me you'll come home every summer," said Hannah.

"That I will and you'll come to us as well. You, Dad and Connor have always been there for me and you are my family but it was disconnecting not knowing my heritage."

"I'm trying to understand, really I am and now so far away___"

"Be glad for us and be thankful for me that I found my mother."

"You're right. I'm being selfish. John and I will be your first visitors."

"Good."

Peter circled his arm around Hannah's shoulder and she rested her head on his.

The Carlsons left to return home to Boston. Peter told them he would keep them informed of their progress. Again a new family had been created by blood, adoption and love.

A year later Peter, Ellen, Liam and Fiona were on their way to a new life in America.

Chapter Twenty One

∼

"We better take two cars to pick up Peter and his family. Sounds like they have brought everything they own," said Joe.

"Well they are moving here."

"Yes, I know. I'll be in the station wagon. You can follow me to Logan."

Maggie and Joe greeted Peter and his family and headed toward the baggage claim. They had six suitcases and a large trunk. After clearing customs they headed home.

Ellen could not believe her good fortune. *Everything is big; cars, buildings, houses and people. I must find work here and not in a book store.*

Joe and Maggie drove into the driveway of their four bedroom colonial and again Ellen was amazed. Maggie gave Ellen and the children a quick tour while Joe and Peter carried the luggage to the basement which was to be their home until they found something.

"Joe worked hard to get this place livable for you," said Maggie as they descended into the basement. Ellen surveyed her surroundings; a large living room, two small bedrooms and a bathroom. Their luggage took up all the space in the living room.

Ellen was stunned, Peter was grateful and Liam and Fiona jumped all over the furniture.

Peter's company found him a position in Boston and he would start his job the following week leaving Ellen to care for the children and spend her days in the basement.   Dinner was chaotic the first week. Liam and Fiona fussed about the food and insisted on sitting next to their parents. Ellen would retreat outside forgoing food for a cigarette. Peter tried to smooth things over by thanking Maggie and Joe for having them. The dishwasher was run through twice a day and the washer and dryer were in continual use.

Often Joe and Maggie would hear the heated voices of Peter and Ellen coming from the basement.

"They need to find a place soon," said Joe.

"I'm sure they will. It's only been two weeks. It takes time to get to know it here."

"Two weeks! Feels like two months. I'll be late tonight don't wait dinner for me."

One evening they sat down together to enjoy a roast chicken dinner that Maggie had prepared. Maggie fixed a plate, covered it with tin foil and placed it on the counter for Joe who would not be dining with them again.

"I think I'll start making the meal on Saturday nights. How does that sound?" asked Peter.

"Does it have to be ham and cabbage?" asked Emma.

"I think I'll be out those nights," laughed Frances."

"I think it's a fine suggestion. Might learn something about Irish cooking," said Maggie.

"My mother made the best Irish bread and served it hot with loads of butter and good tea," said Peter.

"How about hot chocolate for Liam and Fiona with melted marshmallows?" asked Maggie.

"Can we Daddy?" asked Liam.

"Of course. I'll have one too."

"I'll make it for all of us," said Maggie.

"Count me out," said Ellen as she rose cleared her plate and headed downstairs.

Emma and Frances chatted with Liam and Fiona, Peter cleared the table and Maggie made hot chocolate for all of them.

Joe arrived home after the others had gone to bed and ate his dinner in front of the television set.

Frances was working and looking for an apartment; Emma had just completed her degree and was looking for a teaching job. They had a natural refinement about them. They were polite but had their opinions, deferred to their parents where matters of running the house were concerned and enjoyed being together. They had their own bedrooms while Ellen shared her small living space with three others.

Ellen looked at Peter who had fallen asleep in front of their television set.

"Peter," she nudged him. "Wake up."

"I need to find work, I'm bored. You go to work every day and all I do is sit in this basement and when I do go upstairs all Maggie talks about is you and Liam and Fiona. And every one works, even Emma has found a job.""

"You're the one that wanted to move here, what did you think would happen? That we would buy a big house and have a big yard. Those things take time and money."

"I am sick of your indifference to me. All you care about is Maggie."

"Why don't I drive you to the motor vehicle registry to get your permit and I'll teach you to drive. Then you can take me to work, use the car, take the kids to school and get to meet people. I do care about Maggie but I love you and the kids."

"Well show it and find us a place, now. Or better yet I'll get a job and find us place of our own."

Ellen flew up the stairs and ran into Maggie.

"Ellen, care to join me in a cup of tea."

"No. How would you like to babysit if I got a job? Liam is in school all day and Fiona can go to kindergarten mornings or afternoons."

"Have you talked to Peter about this?"

"Peter, Peter, Peter. That's all I hear. Will you think about it?"

"Yes."

Ellen returned downstairs.

"I'm going to sleep on the couch in the living room upstairs tonight."

"Fine," said Peter.

The holidays were over and 1990 had begun. The family had been in America for six weeks during which time Peter and Maggie continued developing their relationship as mother and son. They discussed their fondness for books, movies and TV, and their dislike for some politicians.

On the nights Joe arrived home late he would hang up his coat, remove the tin foil from his plate, pour himself a beer, read the paper and eat his dinner alone. Most nights Ellen stayed in the basement poring over her driver's handbook and reading *Ladies Home Journal.*

Maggie, humming a tune, had just come up from the basement with a basket of laundry. Ellen was seated at the kitchen table, thumbing through a magazine.

"Would you like to cook dinner tonight, Ellen?"

Ellen continued looking at the magazine. "No, I wouldn't. You seem to enjoy it, so why don't you do it. Liam and Fiona like what you make and now they are raving about Peter's meals."

Maggie hesitated, and then said. "Look, Ellen..." That's as far as she got.

Ellen slapped the magazine down on the table. "Your girls are working and looking for apartments and I am supposed to cook for them."

Maggie arched her eyebrows.

"And take care of my children when they come home from school. Then I have to listen to all of you go on about how great it is for us to be together." She stood up and folded her arms. "I've decided to look for a job. Liam and Fiona have taken to you anyway, so you can look after them until I get home."

Stunned, Maggie raised her hand. Momentarily, Ellen thought she had gone too far but caught her breath and continued. "You work mornings so it should fit into your schedule."

"I'll help you and Peter anyway I can..." Maggie stopped and slammed the basket down. "Coming here was Peter's and your idea. We are helping all we can. Everyone is adjusting as best we can; now you better get on board. We've opened up our home to you. Have you no sense of gratitude?"

"Gratitude for what, living in a basement?"

"Yes. We're a family. Do you have any idea what that means?"

"A family! You're so taken up with your son, you can't see anything else." Ellen tossed her hair. "I'll take my driver's test and when I get my license I'll start to look for work. By the way I notice Joe isn't always around." And with that she left the room.

"Joe...Joe" Maggie uttered.

Had she ignored him? Did he feel left out? When was the last time they spent time even moments talking? When was the last time they made love?

Maggie snapped the towels folded them and tossed them into the laundry basket along with unmatched socks.

How could Ellen think this way? Had Maggie been inconsiderate of other people since renewing her life with her son? Who or what was the cause of Ellen's anger? Does she love Peter? Are the living conditions that unsuitable? Maggie thought being together with her family and Peter's family would be a natural blend, separate but reaching out to each other for love and support, Maggie was so sure it would work but she did not count on Ellen's dissatisfaction.

The door opened and Peter walked in. "Maggie, you look distraught. Are you alright?"

She stood up and brushed her hair away from her face. "I'm fine. How was work?"

"Good, I received an evaluation. Got a raise. Ellen and I will be looking for a place of our own.

"That's great. You'll all be glad to get out of the basement."

"Yes, it is getting a little cramped, but we are grateful for everything you've done for us. Are you sure you're alright?"

"Yes, I'm fine," she answered hiding her balled fist behind her back.

Ellen searched the newspapers for apartments to rent. She circled several which she and Peter set out to see the following Saturday. They chose a place halfway from Maggie's house and Ethan's work in a suburb of Boston. They packed up their belongings, moved into their apartment and started life on their own.

Ellen passed her driver's test, drove Peter to work two mornings a week and looked for work. There were numerous opportunities for employment in towns so close to Boston. Ellen would ask to see the person in charge, and with a broad smile and firm handshake introduce herself.

"Hello, I'm Ellen Shea, just here from Ireland, looking for employment. I've seen your ad in the newspaper and I was impressed. Now then, would you be looking for someone to help out around here? I'm dependable and can do almost anything if I'm given a chance." She was too good to be true.

Most employers were taken aback by her formidable introduction and those that did not have an opening wished they did. Some referred her to other places. She was hired by a small law firm to answer the phone, make appointments, do some filing and keep the coffee pot full. She accepted the position without discussion as to what would happen at home. She would figure that out later.

Peter arrived home from work and before his jacket was hung up, Ellen approached, with her hands on her hips, and blurted out, "I have a job with a law firm in town and I start next week. I have it all figured out. I can ride the bus and Maggie can babysit."

Peter's mouth hung open. His jacket hung limp over his arm, "I knew you were looking but shouldn't we have discussed it first, especially with the kids?"

"Maggie is willing to mind the kids and we can pick them up at her house after work. Or you can because I'll be taking the bus."

"And what happens in the summer when school is out?" He threw his jacket on the chair. "Is this five days a week?"

"Yes, nine to five. This was too good to pass up. We'll figure out the summer when it happens. I knew Maggie would do it. I see how happy Liam and Fiona are with her and how she loves them."

"Don't ever make a decision like that again until we discuss it. Understand?"

"Understood." But Ellen had what she wanted.

Maggie did not discuss with Joe the discourse she and Ellen had, preferring to put it out of her mind at least for now. Peter picked up the children up after work at Maggie's and on Friday would stay for dinner. Ellen would join them but spent most of her time on the telephone.

"Had a late lunch, eat without me," she stated. Gradually her appearances withered until she didn't come at all. There was no mention of her absence.

One evening Joe asked where she was. Peter shrugged his shoulders.

"She's probably tired from working all week and needs some time to herself, that's all," Maggie said. "Liam, how was school today?"

"Seems to me we all need time for ourselves," Joe said as he threw his napkin on the table and walked off to the living room.

"Maybe we should not come every Friday__"

"No, no. Joe's just tired. He'll be fine. Now let's have dessert before you leave."

Hearing that conversation, Joe grabbed his coat and left the house. Maggie was asleep when he arrived back and never noticed until morning that he slept in Emma's old room.

Ellen's long dark hair fell around her shoulders, her lips were defined by red lipstick that made them appear fuller, her eyes were bright and her voice had an alluring lilt to it; but most of all her manner was appealing. She walked straight, held her head up high and sat with one leg over the other with her arms resting on her knee. She made the most of her wardrobe which consisted of blouses and sweaters that enhanced her curves and skirts that showed off her shapely legs enhanced by high heels. She was luscious to look at and listen to which did not go unnoticed at work.

Summer arrived with its eighty degree weather. Emma was teaching and had summers off. She was only too glad to bring her sister and brother to the local pond for a swim followed by ice cream at Benny's. More often than not the children would happily stay overnight with Maggie and Joe.

Emma taught Fiona her letters and read a bedtime story to her every night. Maggie read to Liam until he fell asleep.

Toward Christmas, Peter had a bout of illness he couldn't shake. Fatigue, body aches and loss of appetite. The doctor could not find anything amiss. Ellen was unperturbed and Maggie urged him to see another doctor which he avoided doing.

"Get some rest. Leave the children at Maggie's for the weekend. I've got some things to catch up on." Ellen told Peter.

Maggie was used to the children showing up unexpectedly to spend the weekend so this was no different. Joe, however, never got used to it. His plan of a movie and dinner with Maggie often did not materialize. Maggie shrugged it off and Joe went to the movie unaccompanied.

One Friday night after work, William, one of the lawyers, was going to a local bar with some of his coworkers and invited Ellen to come along. Her boredom had reached its capacity and she yearned for some excitement. This seemed innocent enough and she accepted William's offer to drive her. This single incident became routine. William and Ellen left work every Friday together to stop at the bar for a drink and soon they drifted away from the others and went off on their own. Ellen was enamored of William and the prospect of their weekly rendezvous excited her. She was paying less attention at home and more on her looks and attire.

William had noticed her the first day she came to work and the wedding band on her left hand did not deter him. One night he offered to drive her home and took her to the local park where he made advances that she did not resist, in fact, she responded to his warm kisses by kissing him back.

Peter's exhaustion peaked on Fridays and he hardly noticed Ellen's late arrivals. He was usually asleep on the sofa when she came home.

One night Ellen sat in the living room in the dark. *They will hate me by what I am about to do, but Liam and Fiona are happy with the Carlsons and Peter has Maggie and Maggie is happy with all of it. So maybe it won't be too bad. It's not like I am leaving them without anyone.*

Peter arrived home late; the children were with Maggie for the weekend. He walked in the front door and saw a suitcase in the living room with Ellen's coat and jacket draped over it.

"Ellen. Ellen," he called.

She walked into the living room straight over to Peter and stared at him. Peter's stomach clenched. He reached for her; she pulled back and held up her hand.

"I'm sorry. I can't stay any longer. This is not for me."

Peter couldn't speak. He couldn't move. He stared at her. His heart pounded, beads of sweat broke out along his forehead.

"But...why? Where are you going? Ellen, you can't just leave. I love you. You're my wife and what about the kids? I know what it means to lose a mother but not like this. Please, don't go, for their sake."

She hesitated for a moment. "Sorry, my mind's made up." She grabbed her things and headed out the door.

Chapter Twenty Two

❧

Maggie woke as Joe was pulling on his trousers before heading downstairs to answer the door.

"Who can that be?" she mumbled glancing at the clock.

"I don't know, but whoever it is they are persistent."

Joe sprinted downstairs, looked through the glass in the door and saw Peter. He hesitated before unlocking the door and opening it. Maggie was at the top of the stairs and witnessed Peter falling into Joe's arms. She flew down the stairs and they helped him get to the couch in the living room. Joe positioned him and Maggie ran to get a damp cloth and a glass of water.

"I'm all right now. Just let me stay for a bit," Peter said, placing his head on the back of the couch.

"What happened?" Joe asked.

With tears rimming his eyes, he looked at Joe. "She's gone, Joe. Ellen's gone."

"She's gone? Where?"

Maggie entered the room and hearing this she rushed toward Peter.

"I don't know. Said our life is not for her."

Joe threw his hands in the air, turned and faced the window.

"Oh Peter," Maggie said as she dabbed his face. "She'll come to her senses. She'll come back. There's Liam and Fiona. And you're a family. She's probably going through something. But she'll come back, you'll see. Won't she, Joe?" She didn't take her eyes off Peter. "Besides, where would she go? She'll probably be back in the morning. You'll see. She'll come back, won't she, Joe?" She wiped her cheek with the back of her hand. Peter placed his head down on the arm of the couch and lifted his legs.

"I need to rest. I'm tired." His eyes had a blank stare. Maggie sat on the edge of the couch, pushed the collar of his jacket away from his neck, turned to retrieve the glass of water and knocked it over, its contents spilled over the floor. She righted the glass and turned back to Peter, whose eyes were closed. She dabbed his face with the wet cloth. Her eyes darted around the living room looking for Joe who stood with his arms folded staring out of the window at the black sky. Rain was starting to fall.

"Joe, close the curtains," Maggie said as she turned on the lamps at either end of the couch. She removed Peter's shoes, placed a pillow under his head and covered him with a blanket. She sat at the edge of the couch. Joe climbed the stairs and silently closed their bedroom door.

Maggie looked at her son.

How can I make this right for him? Maybe none of this would have happened if I kept him. He would have married someone here, gone to school here and not have all the stress of losing his mother and the search...the search to find me. If only I had known what havoc would be wrought upon him...if only I had known? But if I kept him, where would we be now? I can see what problems we would have encountered back then. She stood up and wrapped her robe around her. *The children are asleep and their mother has left them but I will make sure they are cared for and loved.*

"We'll figure all this out in the morning," she said as she kissed Peter's forehead.

Maggie entered the darkened bedroom where Joe was on his side facing away from the door.

"Joe."

No answer. Maggie removed her robe and slipped under the covers. Joe closed his eyes.

The following morning Emma, Liam and Fiona were in the kitchen eating cereal when Maggie walked in. Peter followed shortly after.

"Mom, you look like you've been up all night. Too much late night TV," quipped Emma.

Peter spoke first. "Liam and Fiona. I have some news," he said, remembering when his father told him his mother had died.

"Mom's gone away for a while."

"Where did she go?' asked Liam. Fiona started to cry.

Peter picked up Fiona and held her on his lap. "I'm not sure just yet. She'll call and let us know where she is." Peter struggled with the words.

"Did you give her a ride, somewhere?" Liam asked, remembering his mother didn't have a car.

Peter thought for a moment. She was packed at that late hour. Was she expecting someone?

"No I didn't, Liam." He held Fiona close and pulled Liam over to him. "Now, you'll stay here with Maggie and Joe and Emma tonight and tomorrow we'll return home. Maggie or I will pick you up at school every day."

"I don't want to go to school. I want Mommy."

"Me too," said Liam.

"I'm sure she'll be calling the two of you soon and she'll be asking about school," said Emma. "I feel sad that she's gone, too."

"You're not going away, are you, Daddy?" asked Liam.

"No," Peter smiled. "I'm not."

"And neither are any of us." Maggie said.

Joe finished his coffee, grabbed his briefcase and headed out the door.

Ethan arrived with a box of *Time* magazines. He was an ardent subscriber.

"Thought I'd drop these off on my way to work, see if anyone wants them. Did I come at a bad time? You all look like you're coming down with something."

"Ethan, Ellen has gone away. We don't know where she is but we are sure she will call," said Maggie. She stared at Ethan who got the message.

"Right. I'll just leave these for whoever wants them."

"I'll take them," said Peter. "We can put them in my car."

Peter and Ethan walked out and Peter told him the full story.

"I thought everything was going great. I guess we really don't know how a person feels inside. I'm sorry Peter. It must be tough for you and the kids. How is Maggie with all of this?"

"We are still reeling but things will calm down. We have the rest of the weekend to figure it out." Ethan placed the boxes in the trunk of Peter's car where they remained, forgotten.

Two weeks went by without a word from Ellen. The children spent weekends with Maggie and Joe. Peter went home to sit by the phone to wait for a call from Ellen which never came.

Peter could wait no longer. He drove to the building where Ellen worked and walked in the front door. He glanced at a glass enclosed directory to look for the office where she worked. Finding the number he hit the elevator button. The doors opened and several people stepped off. Peter caught a glimpse of one of them. A hint of familiarity caused Peter to stare and when the man turned left toward the exit he realized the man was William Duxbury. His mind raced. *It can't be but it is too much of a coincidence.* A passenger stepped onto the elevator and asked if anyone was going up. Peter got on. By the time Peter arrived at the office where Ellen worked he was totally disarmed. He paced up and down the corridor several times forcing him to remember why he was there and to erase William's face from his mind. Finally, he reined in his anger, regained his composure and opened the office door. Ellen was on the phone.

"I need to talk to talk to you, now."

Ellen placed her hand over the phone. "Can't you see? I'm busy?"

"Finish the conversation and let's go in the corridor."

Ellen slammed the phone down and pushed her chair away from the desk. She followed Peter into the corridor. He leaned against the wall looking at the woman he once loved and saw defiance in her eyes.

"No call, not even to the kids. I need to know what you intend to do?" he asked.

"I want a divorce."

"Who's the guy?"

"You don't know him."

"Tell me his name anyway."

"William Duxbury."

Peter's mind reeled.

"Did you say William Duxbury?"

"Yes, he went to Trinity College but finished here, unlike you who never graduated."

The words collided in his brain with his sense of loyalty and commitment. How did this happen? Where did it go wrong? What did he do or not do?

Ellen folded her arms and stood with both feet together.

"You can have your divorce but you'll never get Liam and Fiona."

Ellen turned walked into the office and closed the door.

A year later Peter was a single parent with custody of his two children. Ellen saw them every other weekend but not overnight. Her new husband, William Duxbury, would not allow it.

Friday night became pizza night. Peter, Liam, Fiona, Emma, Frances and Ethan would arrive with three large pizzas for Maggie and Joe. Occasionally Maggie's father would show up with a ham sandwich to protest pizza which he detested.

On one such Friday night the weather turned foul. Wind was driving the rain sideways, claps of thunder roared overhead and the crackle of lightening lit up the dark sky. Peter's mood matched the weather as he told the family of a change at his job. He was being transferred to another department because they wanted to move ahead with research and development and found a more suitable candidate, an MIT graduate with more experience in the field. It was totally unexpected. The voices of reassurance did nothing to lift Peter's spirits.

Much to Maggie's insistence they stay with her and Joe, Peter and Ethan decided to go home but Frances, Emma, Liam and Fiona stayed overnight. Maggie waved goodbye and yelled to them to call when they arrived home. They left in separate cars. Peter turned on his windshield wipers and the only one working was on the driver's side. "Damn" he shouted aloud. He backed down the driveway, turned and headed home. The loss and failure he felt as a husband never quite left him and to think William Duxbury held a grudge against him for so long and that he was able to alienate Ellen's affections for him. The situation at his job grated on him. Sobs wracked his body and tears flooded his cheeks. Only one windshield wiper helped him see his way as he brushed tears from his face with the cuff of his jacket. A tree branch blew across the stop sign obliterating his view; he braked too late and slid across the intersection. The oncoming truck smashed Peter's car broadside almost cutting it in two, *Time* magazines were strewn about the road.

The truck driver staggered to the curb and sat dazed, confused and soaking wet, a bloody gash on his forehead. When the police arrived, they approached him first and covered him with a plastic raincoat advising him not to move. One officer stayed with him while the other one approached the mangled vehicle. The inclement weather made it impossible to determine where the body was. Within minutes two rescue trucks arrived and a second police car. Two medics unloaded a gurney and whisked the truck driver away while the other medics turned their attention to the car holding Peter's remains. Another rescue truck arrived on the scene. The police cars shone their lights on the car while the medics tried desperately to reach the body through shattered glass, snarled metal and blood. Peter was crushed by the compacted vehicle trapping him inside. The medics kept working until they freed Peter's broken, lifeless body. They placed him in the ambulance and roared away sirens blasting to the nearest hospital. The police surveyed the scene and directed traffic which began to pile up. One of the policemen called in the car registration and was given Peter's name, address and telephone number. He dialed the number but no one was there to pick up the telephone. The other policeman lifted several *Time* magazines from the road, brought them inside his car and was able to decipher Ethan's name and address. The pair drove to the Ethan's home, rang the bell and waited.

Ethan, watching television, wondered who could be out on a terrible night and at this hour. He opened the door and before the police could finish speaking Ethan swayed, his mind couldn't fathom the words... "accident...Peter Shea...do you know him... taken to the hospital...bad condition..." One of the policemen stepped into the entry and held Ethan's arm. Together the officers sat him down, made coffee and waited for Ethan to digest the tragedy.

They offered to drive him to the hospital which he accepted. Hoping for the best and dreading the worst he waited until a doctor arrived with news that Ethan did not want to hear. Peter was dead. At first Ethan shook his head trying to make sense of what he just heard. He waited for more but there was no more, nothing was left but the finality of death.

"I must tell my sister. I have to go to her."

The officers offered to drive Ethan to Maggie's.

Ethan unlocked the front door to Maggie's house and let himself in. His shoes left a puddle on the floor of the front hall; he tore off his jacket and dropped it. It was five o'clock in the morning. Shaking from head to foot, he attempted to clear the mixture of tears and rain on his face with his shirt tail but it was no use, more tears came. He was unable to move. Maggie stirred, she thought she heard something but wasn't sure. She threw off the covers and went to the top of the stairs. Ethan looked up and he held his hands open while grief enveloped his face.

"It's Peter...an accident..." he shrieked. "I'm so sorry."

Maggie let out a wail that could shatter glass. The officers entered the house and closed the door as Joe flew downstairs followed by the rest of the family.

There was much to do, details to be attended to and funeral arrangements, because of this Maggie stored her grief away until enough time passed when she could think about it and let it overwhelm her. She mothered Liam, who would speak only to her and Fiona, who cried constantly. They were at her side during the day and they slept in her room at night. Maggie moved slowly acknowledging those around her with minimal responses. Every morning she woke at five o'clock, lifted herself out of bed and stood looking out at the darkness. She made breakfast for Liam and Fiona and told them Daddy would want them to remember him and it was okay to cry and be sad.

Maggie spoke in short crisp sentences. A veil of loss enveloped her. She asked Ethan to order food which no one ate, she asked Joe to call Donal in Ireland and turned her attention to her son's funeral arrangements.

Joe dialed the number in Ireland forgetting the time difference. Hannah and her husband were awaiting their first born, due any day. Listening to the ring he waited and thought about all that happened to the family.

Donal answered. "Hello."

"Donal, it's Joe."

"Joe, now what would you be calling me about at this late hour? It can't be good."

"It's not," Joe said as he revealed the bad news.

Donal slumped into the chair. "He's with my Julia, his mother. They say when a life is taken another will be born which in this case two have been born; Hannah and her husband had twins, a boy and girl, born two hours ago. We welcome birth, and we mourn for our dead and we cannot avoid either of them, each in its own time; still tis a pity of enormous proportion losing one so young and so much loved. I'll let Hannah and her husband bask with their new babes before I tell them; in the meantime I'll do my own mourning for the loss of my son."

Joe heard a quiver in Donal's voice.

"I am so sorry, Donal. Peter's death has affected all of us. My condolences to you and Hannah and my congratulations as well. I'm sure Maggie will call when she is ready. We have a lot of help here. Maggie has taken over the kids and insists on making the funeral arrangements but Ethan and I are at her side if she needs us and the girls are trying any way they can to help out. At least I'll have some good news to pass on to the family."

"I'll not come right now, maybe later when the weather is better. Give Maggie my condolences and thank her for everything she did for my son. I can't talk anymore, Joe, I am empty of words."

"I understand. I'll give Maggie the message," Joe answered.

Tom and Richard parked outside the house. Tom got out of the car first, adjusted his tie and straightened his shoulders. Richard shifted in his seat then stood and with a grim look on his face and slumped shoulders followed Tom into the house. Maggie and Richard clung to each other which was all they could do. Unable and afraid to let his anguish lose, Tom grasped Maggie's hands. All she saw was utter sadness and the absence of tears.

The funeral was held the following Monday. Ellen sat in the back row of church and waited until all the mourners filed out, hoping no one would notice her. She followed them to the cemetery and sat in the car as Peter was laid to rest. Joe bent his head to Maggie's ear and looked towards Ellen's car. When the service was over they walked to Ellen's car and invited her back to their house for refreshments which she accepted.

The dining room table was set with sandwiches, cookies, fruit, cold drinks and a coffee pot. Friends came by to offer condolences and offer help in any way they could.

Ellen refused Ethan's offer for food and coffee and kept her coat wrapped around her.

Maggie drew Liam and Fiona close to her and said, "Mommy and I are going to talk in the den. We won't be long. This way, Ellen."

Refusing Maggie's offer to sit Ellen stood arms folded still clinging to her coat.

"After the divorce Peter had a lawyer draw up his will giving me full custody of the children in case of his death. You will have visitation rights on weekends just as it says in the divorce papers. If you harm the children in any way or if I think they are fearful of going to you that will change. Do you understand?"

"It was always about you and him. Wasn't it?"

"If you mean we loved and cared for each other...yes. Someday I hope you know what that means."

"I have someone, so I do know what that means."

"I'm glad for you. Now if you will excuse me. Ethan will show you the way out.

Mourners left with words: "call me if you need anything," "this will pass," "you will be stronger," "you have the children to think of." All well-intentioned but useless to Maggie who wanted to scream, "Why was he taken from me again!"

During the night Maggie rose, went to the window and looked out. It was dark, no rain, and no wind, just dark. Dark as her grief. The pain of loss was relentless. She saw Peter in Liam and Fiona, she saw him at the dinner table, she remembered the first time she saw him at the airport. Friday nights were unbearable. She sobbed into her hands. Joe woke up went to her and wrapped his arms around her. They held each silently and continued to cry together.

Chapter Twenty Three

❧

Ethan had just arrived at work and his telephone rang. It was Maggie insisting he take her to the site of the accident.

"Are you sure you want to do this?"

"Yes, it's been three weeks and I need to do this."

They drove to the crash site; Maggie got out of the car and walked over to the stop sign which had been cleared of obstacles. Ethan stood at her side.

"I should have insisted he stay with us that night. That's all I had to do," she yelled.

"Peter made up his own mind. It's not your fault, Maggie. C'mon let's go."

"It's all my fault. For getting pregnant, for giving him away and letting him go that night."

"Maggie, you have to stop this. None of us are responsible for decisions others make.We are all human and we decide what is best for us. Some of it is good, some of it is bad but it is ours. We fail or we succeed."

"I wait for him to come through the door on Friday nights. I still can't believe he's gone. I've lost him again!"

"Why don't we start having pizza again on Friday night? Let's get back to doing things we did before Peter's death."

"But he won't be there!" she cried.

"Look it will take time to get over his death but we will not get over loving Peter."

Gradually Maggie came to terms with Peter's death and took a renewed interest in daily activities, all of which was around Liam and Fiona, their school, homework, friends, and errands for them. The pain would never go away but she began to function normally. Loosing Peter was part of her life but not the center.

Six months later Maggie and Joe had legal custody of twelve year old Liam and nine year old Fiona whose lives would not be uprooted again if Maggie had anything to do with it. Ellen's visits on Saturday or Sunday became infrequent. Something always came up. Liam played baseball and developed friends whom he spent time with on the weekend. His mother's visits were complicated. Fiona started sleepovers which usually occurred on Friday nights interfering with Ellen's visits on Saturday. Slowly Ellen's visits stopped, her phone calls became sparse and her birthday cards arrived late if at all.

Maggie thought she had a blueprint for family life, the one she and Joe had created with Frances and Emma. This was different. Phone calls interrupted family dinners, Fiona needed a ride to a sleepover, and Liam needed to be picked up after baseball.

Their friends came over on the weekend to watch television, devour pizza and were dropped off by parents twenty years younger than Maggie and Joe. Joe's private time disappeared and his time with Maggie became obsolete.

Dinner time was chaotic. Liam and Fiona developed fast eating habits and had no time for chatting with Maggie and Joe. They had to be reminded to clear their plates, and tidy their rooms that looked like six people lived there. Maggie had gone back to work part time to be at home when Liam and Fiona arrived from school. Often she would get a call at work that Liam was going to Eric's house and could she pick him up at five o'clock. Fiona would arrive home with her friend take the platter of brownies and would retreat upstairs to her bedroom to listen to the latest hit tunes. Maggie was left alone

Joe was getting tired of stepping over boots and shoes in the hallway when he came home from work. The phone rang constantly and music blared from the bedrooms. Sometimes no one was there; Maggie was picking up kids and doing last minute errands, mainly for them.

One Saturday night Joe went to the freezer to get his favorite ice cream. The container was in the sink, empty. The next morning he arrived in the kitchen to see six kids finishing off the last of the orange juice and the last of the cereal. Empty pizza boxes were strewn about on the kitchen counter. Liam looked up, greeted Joe and went on gabbing with his friends.

Joe went back upstairs and met Maggie coming down. "I need to talk to you."

They entered their bedroom and Joe closed the door.

"First it was Peter and his family encroaching on us, then Ellen takes a hike and you fill that hole. Peter's death was hard on all of us especially you and the kids but they are taking over. I don't mind but there are limits. They are in the driver's seat and we are in the trunk. We have inherited a family after we finished raising ours. We never go out. We never have a dinner together. There are always interruptions. We haven't had a vacation in four years. Are you aware of that? Or has it not crossed your mind? I loved our life before Peter and I want it back. I want you back. Have you even thought of what I am thinking or what I want?"

"Of course. I think of you all the time."

"Since when?" Joe's raised voice was shaking.

Maggie watched in horror as he tossed some things in a suitcase. "Joe, what are you doing?"

"I need some time to sort things out."

"Joe, don't leave. I love you. I can't live without you. Please."

"I'll call you." Joe stomped down the stairs, hurried out of the house and drove away.

Maggie followed calling after him to come back.

Was Joe denied admittance to Maggie and Peter's inner circle? Did she unknowingly exclude him? She never stopped loving him that she was sure of but was her love was misplaced by events she had no control over or did she? She sifted the ashes of her life in her mind remembering the intense feeling of excitement she felt for Joe in the beginning of their relationship which never left. Was Joe being selfish? Did he understand how Maggie felt about her son?

I'll give him time if that is what he needs. He said he would call and I'll wait.

Maggie continued caring for Liam and Fiona but rearranged their social life. Friday night was sleepover, one friend each. Sports would continue but she arranged car pools. They would come home after school every day except when Maggie gave her approval to go to a friend's house or have a friend over. It was time to free herself of guilt, sadness and regret and become a fully integrated person which meant taking charge of her life. Liam and Fiona's activities were scrutinized. If they didn't fit into Maggie's schedule the activity would have to wait. Chores were listed on the fridge for Liam and Fiona to accomplish.

"If we do this will Joe come back?" asked Fiona.

"Maybe," Maggie laughed. "He didn't like having his favorite ice cream disappear."

"I wouldn't like that either," said Liam.

"Is it our fault that he left? I wish Daddy never died," said Fiona.

"It's not your fault and, yes, I wish Daddy didn't die either. Maybe if Joe told me what was bothering him we could have talked about it, like we are doing now. You have to tell people how you feel and maybe if I paid more attention to him he would not have left."

"Yeah, maybe if I knew he wanted some ice cream, I would have saved him some."

"What we do and say are important and we don't want to hurt anyone but sometime it happens and when it does we need to forgive ourselves and try to do better next time."

"When he comes back I'll clean my room," said Fiona.

"And I will ask him to talk to me and pay more attention to him," said Maggie.

Two weeks later Maggie was sorting mail in the kitchen when the door opened. Joe stepped in and dropped his suitcase on the floor. She thought she would jump out of her skin instead she wrapped her arms around him and he buried his face in her hair.

"Can you forgive me?"

"Yes, I can."

Epilogue

◈

Maggie stepped out of the shower, slipped into her pajamas and bathrobe and towel dried her hair. She glanced in the mirror at her vibrant look even with traces of gray hair appearing around her temples. She would think about that later, she thought, brushing her hair, covering the unwanted change.

She left and stopped by the next bedroom to peek in on Liam, who was fast asleep. He was content these days, had a full life as full as any teenager could have. She pulled the covers around him and kissed him on his forehead, left the room and headed for the next bedroom where Fiona slept with her arms around her pink bunny. Maggie adjusted the quilt and kissed her.

It had been two years since Peter's death.

Downstairs Joe was snoozing on the couch. The television was on with the sound low. Maggie went into the kitchen and made herself a cup of tea. When she entered the living room Joe roused from his light slumber. She sat beside him and planted a soft kiss on his lips.

"What should we do this weekend?" she asked.

"I thought we'd rent a movie, make popcorn and ask Liam and Fiona to join us."

"Sounds wonderful. And if they don't want to you've got a date."

"I'll get a bottle of wine and we may even get a pizza. The pizza may attract the kids."

"That's fine. We've come a long way together, Joe."

"Yes, we have."

Maggie thought of Peter's call.

"Does September 2, 1957 mean anything to you?"

It certainly did. All the rest of my days.

Made in the USA
San Bernardino, CA
09 June 2014